THE DEVIL'S PLAYGROUND:
GUARDING OUR KIDS
Against The
INEXPLICABLE

Shawn Sellers & David Humphrey

authorHOUSE

AuthorHouse™
1663 Liberty Drive
Bloomington, IN 47403
www.authorhouse.com
Phone: 833-262-8899

Published by AuthorHouse 07/12/2024

ISBN: 979-8-8230-2962-9 (sc)
ISBN: 979-8-8230-2961-2 (e)

Library of Congress Control Number: 2024913530

Print information available on the last page.

This book is printed on acid-free paper.

Contents

David and I have been inseparable since our earliest memories, bound by a friendship that has endured through thick and thin. Growing up together, we navigated life's twists and turns, and our shared interests led us down some extraordinary paths. As Freemasons and members of various Masonic organizations, we've embraced the values of brotherhood and service. Our mutual fascination with the unknown propelled us into the realms of the paranormal, UFOs, mysteries, and the occult. We've crisscrossed the United States, delving into cold cases, abduction stories, and monster sightings, always seeking the truth behind the inexplicable.

Our investigative journeys have not gone unnoticed. We've been honored guests on numerous podcasts and even hosted our own for many years, sharing our findings and experiences with an ever-curious audience. Before the COVID-19 pandemic, we brought the supernatural to life through haunted walking tours in our hometown, captivating locals and visitors alike with tales of the eerie and the unexplained.

David is not only a dedicated researcher and investigator; he is also an accomplished author, with this being his second book. His diverse career includes roles as a business owner, a reserve police officer, and the director of an anti-human trafficking organization. His commitment to protecting the vulnerable and fighting for justice is unwavering.

As for myself, I am a researcher, teacher, and coach driven by a passion for uncovering the hidden truths of our world. This book marks the second collaboration between David and me, and it is a testament to our shared dedication to shedding light on the darkest corners of society.

The Devil's Playground: Guarding Our Kids Against Monsters is born from our profound concern for the safety and well-being of our children. In a world where dangers lurk both in the shadows and in plain sight, it is imperative to bring awareness to the threats they face, including the insidious crime of human trafficking. Our book aims to inform, educate, and inspire action. We delve into the chilling realities of human trafficking and other dangers that prey on the innocent, offering insights and strategies to protect those who are most vulnerable.

A personal betrayal unexpectedly prompted our journey into writing this book. David and I had a friend in New Orleans whom I had known since I was fifteen and David since he was eighteen. This friend was a vampire tour guide, and while we were aware of some of the darkness surrounding him, we never imagined how deep it went. We knew of his dabbling in the occult, a side of life most people can't imagine exists, but we never suspected the true extent of his darkness. We were blindsided when he was booked on 150 counts of possession of pornography involving juveniles under the age of 13, according to the Louisiana Attorney General's Office. This horrifying revelation shattered our perceptions and inspired us to write The Devil's Playground.

In today's interconnected world, hidden dangers lurking in the digital landscape threaten children's innocence. As authors, David and I are committed to illuminating these threats and advocating for protecting our most vulnerable members of society. We aim to raise awareness, educate caregivers and young individuals about online safety, and promote proactive measures to safeguard children from online predators.

The digital age has transformed how we connect, learn, and interact. Modern technology has bridged distances, enabling instant communication and access to information. However, this same technology has also become a conduit for those with malicious intent. Online predators exploit social media, messaging apps, and video platforms to identify, groom, and victimize children. This dual nature of technology—its immense potential for good and its capacity for harm—underscores the urgent need for vigilance and education.

Children require stability and safety to thrive and develop properly. Stability provides a sense of predictability and routine essential for their emotional well-being and growth. When children feel safe and secure in their environment, they can better explore, learn, and form healthy relationships. A stable and safe environment includes consistent routines, a secure home, emotional support from caregivers, and protection from harm. Parents and caregivers must create a nurturing environment that fosters children's physical, emotional, and cognitive development.

Despite the best efforts of many parents, the rapid advancement of technology has outpaced traditional methods of supervision and protection. Many caregivers are unaware of the sophisticated techniques predators use to exploit digital platforms. The FBI's studies and statistics reveal that what might seem like a harmless conversation can quickly escalate into something dangerous. The reality is that within minutes, children can receive requests from predators seeking illicit photos and videos. The internet's pervasive nature means that no app or social media platform is entirely safe from these threats.

Parents need to recognize that the dangers of the digital world often surpass those of the physical world. While the idea of a child playing alone in a park can cause worry, the unseen threats online pose an even greater risk. Social media and online applications are now the primary tools predators use to groom and exploit children. These platforms allow predators to masquerade as peers, making it difficult for children to distinguish between friend and foe. The immediacy and anonymity provided by these apps enable predators to manipulate and victimize children with alarming ease.

The advent of AI technology has further complicated this landscape. In the past few months, new AI tools have emerged that can manipulate videos, photos, and even live streams, increasing the potential for exploitation. What a child might consider a harmless post can be twisted into something sinister by predators using advanced technology.

In this book, we will delve into the myriad ways online predators operate, the psychological and emotional impact on victims, and the steps caregivers can take to protect their children. We will share real-life stories, expert insights, and practical advice to help parents and guardians navigate this complex digital terrain. Our goal is to empower readers with the knowledge and resources needed to create a safer online environment for children, fostering a community that prioritizes their well-being and guards against the dangers lurking in the shadows of the internet.

By understanding the risks and implementing effective safety measures, we can transform the digital playground from a potential devil's den into a space where children can safely explore, learn, and connect. Together, we can build a future where childhood innocence is preserved and protected in the digital age.

The issue of child predators is one of the most pressing and severe problems of our digital age. Predators leverage the anonymity and accessibility of the internet to exploit children, leading to long-lasting and often devastating effects on their victims. These effects can include severe psychological trauma, disrupted development, and long-term emotional scars. Victims of online exploitation may struggle with trust issues, anxiety, depression, and even suicidal tendencies. The digital age has created a landscape where the innocence of children can be swiftly corrupted by those with malicious intent, making it imperative for society to take action.

This book introduces the "Devil's Playground" concept as a powerful metaphor for the dangers children face online. The term encapsulates the sinister underbelly of the digital world, where predators lurk behind screens, masquerading as friends, peers, or harmless entities. Unlike the physical playgrounds where children play, learn, and grow under the watchful eyes of caregivers, the Devil's Playground is an insidious and hidden realm. The typical safety boundaries are blurred here, and the threats are not immediately visible.

The "Devil's Playground" metaphor highlights the deceptive and hazardous nature of the internet for children. Just as a playground is meant for joy, discovery, and growth, the internet is intended to be a vast resource for learning, socializing, and entertainment. However, within this digital expanse lies a darker dimension where predators manipulate and exploit the innocence of youth. In this playground, the swings and slides are replaced by chat rooms and social media platforms, and the predators' tactics are as varied and sophisticated as the equipment designed to entertain.

Predators employ numerous strategies to groom and exploit children, including posing as peers, engaging in deceptive relationships, and gradually introducing inappropriate content. They exploit the trust and naivety of children, manipulating them into situations that can escalate from seemingly innocent interactions to severe exploitation. The Devil's Playground is a treacherous environment where the typical signs of danger are disguised, making it crucial for parents and caregivers to be vigilant and informed.

Raising awareness about child predators and their tactics is essential in combating this issue. Many parents and caregivers remain unaware of the sophisticated methods predators use to target children. These methods can include befriending children online, building trust over time, and manipulating them into sharing personal information or explicit content. By understanding these tactics, parents can better equip themselves to protect their children.

Education and awareness campaigns are vital in highlighting the risks and promoting safe online practices. Parents must understand that their children's daily devices can be gateways for predators. Predators exploit social media platforms, messaging apps, and even seemingly harmless games to gain access to potential victims. As technology continues to evolve, so do the methods these malicious individuals use, making ongoing education and vigilance crucial.

The impact of online exploitation on victims is profound and multifaceted. Children who fall prey to predators often experience intense feelings of shame, guilt, and fear. They may blame themselves for the abuse, leading to deep-seated emotional and psychological issues. These kids may suffer from anxiety, depression, PTSD, and a variety of other mental health issues. The trauma can also affect their academic performance, social interactions, and overall development.

The long-term effects can extend into adulthood, where victims might struggle with forming healthy relationships, maintaining employment, and achieving personal and professional goals. The sense of violation and betrayal can linger for years, impacting every aspect of their lives. As a result, we must handle this problem with the urgency and gravity it requires for our immediate safety and long-term well-being.

Protecting children from the dangers of the Devil's Playground requires a multifaceted approach. It involves educating children about the risks and empowering them to recognize and report inappropriate behavior. Parents and caregivers must be proactive in monitoring their children's online activities, setting boundaries, and fostering open lines of communication. Additionally, tech companies, educators, and policymakers must collaborate to create safer online environments and robust reporting mechanisms.

This book will delve deeper into predators' tactics, share real-life stories, and provide practical advice for parents and caregivers. We aim to provide you with the skills and information required to successfully negotiate this complicated digital environment so that the internet remains a resource for learning and development rather than a dangerous haven for predators.

By understanding the issue's seriousness, recognizing the Devil's Playground metaphor, and raising awareness about predators' tactics, we can create a safer digital world for our children. This collective responsibility requires vigilance, education, and a commitment to protecting the most vulnerable members of our society. Together, we can make a difference and safeguard our children's future. Thank you for embarking on this journey with us. May it open your eyes to the realities of our world and motivate you to take action. Welcome to The Devil's Playground.

Educating and Raising Awareness to Safeguard Kids Online

As parents, we need to pay close attention when we give our kids iPads or iPhones, especially when they're alone in their rooms. The online risks can be much more significant than those they encounter playing at the park. One of the most concerning issues is the presence of predators who infiltrate children's inboxes. While it may seem harmless when your child posts something, predators can manipulate these posts and turn them into something dangerous. Across America, there have been numerous cases involving superimposed pornographic images used to lure and extort children.

Former U.S. Attorney David Hickton has highlighted a disturbing trend: predators increasingly target children under 10. This should alarm all parents. Predators often begin by gaining a child's trust through seemingly innocent interactions. This grooming process progresses over time, leading to manipulation and, in some cases, face-to-face meetings. Online games can be an entry point, with innocent conversations evolving into explicit discussions without the child realizing the danger.

While social media offers entertainment, education, and connectedness, it also poses significant risks, especially for younger users. Cyber predators are among the most frightening threats today. As a parent and teacher, I am deeply concerned. Social media can be beneficial, but its darker side necessitates protective measures. In my book, we will explore the dangers of internet predators, privacy invasion, online bullying, and strategies for teaching children about social media. Parental control, supervision, and effective reporting systems are crucial to keeping our kids safe.

Parents must utilize parental controls on devices and apps their children use. Familiarize yourself with these tools and monitor your child's online activity. If an unauthorized app appears, investigate its purpose and your child's interest. Pay attention to warning signs, such as mysterious or secretive behavior. This could indicate something is wrong, and it's time for a serious conversation.

If you suspect something is amiss, don't hesitate to contact law enforcement, religious leaders, or child protection organizations. Everyone must work together to educate and protect our children from online predators. With advancements in artificial intelligence, predators may find it easier to remain hidden. Therefore, we must stay informed and vigilant, collaborate with law enforcement, and continuously improve our strategies.

Parents are the first line of defense. Establish an open relationship with your children so they feel comfortable sharing anything with you, especially if they are in a difficult situation. Remember, while many resources are available, you are your child's primary protector. Together, we can create a safer online environment for our kids.

In today's digital age, the safety of our children is a paramount concern. While a powerful tool for education and entertainment, the internet also harbors significant dangers. Among these are online child predators, who exploit the anonymity and vast reach of the internet to target young, vulnerable individuals. This letter aims to provide a comprehensive understanding of what constitutes a child predator, the tactics they use, and the prevalence of their activities. Increasing awareness and knowledge can better protect our children from these insidious threats.

The digital age has brought numerous benefits but presents significant risks, particularly for children. Online predators are a grave concern, exploiting the anonymity and reach of the internet to target vulnerable young users. Awareness and education are crucial in combating these threats. This paper explores the importance of understanding and education for parents, teachers, caregivers, and children, offering strategies to recognize and respond to predatory behavior.

A child predator is an individual who seeks to exploit children for sexual or other harmful purposes. These predators can be of any age, gender, or background and often operate under the guise of anonymity provided by the internet. They use various tactics to manipulate and exploit children, aiming to build trust and break down barriers before progressing to more explicit and harmful behavior.

Child predators utilize a variety of manipulative tactics to achieve their malicious goals. Understanding these tactics is crucial for recognizing and preventing predatory behavior. This section explores the critical methods used by predators to manipulate and exploit children.

Grooming is a calculated process where predators establish an emotional connection with a child to lower their inhibitions and prepare them for abuse. This process can take place over days, weeks, or even months. During grooming, predators often employ several techniques to build trust and dependency. Predators lavish the children with excessive compliments to make them feel unique and valued. Predators create a sense of obligation and gratitude in the child by giving gifts or favors. Predators provide focused attention, making the child feel understood and appreciated, which can be particularly enticing if the child feels neglected or misunderstood elsewhere. Through these actions, predators slowly break down the child's defenses, making them more susceptible to exploitation. Catfishing involves predators creating fake profiles, often posing as peers or other trustworthy individuals, to gain the child's confidence. This deception allows predators to Appear Relatable by posing as another child or teenager; predators can seem more relatable and trustworthy. Some predators might pose as teachers, coaches, or other authority figures, exploiting the inherent trust associated with these roles. By masquerading as someone else, predators can manipulate children into sharing personal information or engaging in risky behavior.

Isolation is another tactic used by predators to create dependency. They may encourage children to distance themselves from their family and friends, making the child more reliant on the predator for emotional support. Isolation can be achieved through discouraging Interaction, convincing the child that their family or friends don't understand or care about them, thereby driving a wedge between the child and their support system and emphasizing the need to keep their interactions private to maintain control over the child. This isolation makes it easier for predators to manipulate and control the child without interference from their support network.

Desensitization involves gradually exposing the child to sexual content or conversations to normalize such interactions. This tactic aims to lower the child's natural resistance to inappropriate behavior.

Predators may start with seemingly innocent content and progressively introduce more explicit material. Convince the child that sexual discussions or activities are normal and acceptable. By slowly desensitizing the child, predators can make them more accepting of sexual advances.

Once predators obtain compromising material, they often resort to threats and blackmail to maintain control over the child and further exploit them. They are using the fear of exposure to keep the child compliant, such as threatening to share explicit images or conversations with the child's family or friends and threatening harm to the child or their loved ones if they do not comply with the predator's demands. These threats create a powerful tool for predators to ensure the child remains silent and continues to follow their commands.

By understanding these manipulative tactics, parents, caregivers, and educators can better recognize the signs of predatory behavior. Awareness and proactive measures are essential in protecting children from exploitation. The more informed we are about these dangers, the better equipped we will be to safeguard our children's well-being.

Prevalence of Child Predators The threat of child predators is alarmingly prevalent and growing with the expansion of digital communication. Understanding the scope of this issue is crucial for implementing effective protective measures. According to the National Society for the Prevention of Cruelty to Children (NSPCC), one in 25 children aged 10-17 has received an online sexual solicitation. The FBI estimates that there are more than 500,000 predators online each day. While not all online interactions lead to physical abduction, there are disturbing cases where online grooming has escalated to real-life abductions. The National Center for Missing & Exploited Children (NCMEC) reported that online enticement increased by 97.5% from 2019 to 2020.

Case Studies like the Case of Amanda Todd: Amanda Todd was a Canadian teenager who was harassed online by a predator who convinced her to expose herself via a webcam. The predator then used this material to blackmail her, leading to severe bullying and, ultimately, her tragic suicide. The Case of Kayleigh Haywood in the U.K., 15-year-old Kayleigh Haywood was groomed online by a man who then kidnapped and murdered her. This case highlights the potentially deadly consequences of online predation.

Online predators use various tactics to manipulate and exploit children. They often pose as peers to gain trust, gradually introducing inappropriate content or conversations. Predators exploit children's naivety and curiosity, leading them into dangerous situations.

Recognizing Predatory Tactics, parents, teachers, caregivers, and children must be educated about the common tactics predators use. Grooming predators build a relationship with a child, gaining their trust before initiating inappropriate behavior. Catfishing, pretending to be someone else, often another child, to form a deceptive relationship. Exploitation uses threats or blackmail to coerce children into sharing explicit content or meeting in person.

Signs of Predatory Behavior Understanding predatory behavior is crucial for early intervention. Children become secretive about their online activities. They experience sudden changes in behavior, mood, or school performance. They receive gifts or money from unknown sources and spend excessive time online, particularly in private settings.

Educating Parents, Caregivers, and Teachers workshops and Seminars: Regular workshops for parents, caregivers, and teachers on online safety and recognizing predatory behavior. Resource Materials: Access to books, articles, and online resources about internet safety. Parental Controls Training: Training on using parental controls and monitoring software to supervise children's online activities.

Online Safety Curriculum integrates online safety into school curricula, teaching children about the risks and how to navigate the internet safely. Interactive Sessions conduct interactive sessions with children to discuss personal safety, boundaries, and the importance of reporting inappropriate behavior. Role-playing scenarios use role-playing to help children practice responding to potentially dangerous situations online.

Strategies for Open Communication Establishing Trust Open Dialogue encourages an open dialogue where children feel comfortable discussing their online experiences without fear of punishment. Non-judgmental listening is listening to children's concerns without immediate judgment or reprimand, fostering a supportive environment.

Teaching Personal Safety and Boundaries: Setting Clear Rules: Establishing clear rules about internet use, including what information can be shared and with whom. Understanding Consent: Teaching children about consent, personal boundaries, and the importance of saying no to uncomfortable situations. Empowering Children: Empowering children to trust their instincts and report any behavior that makes them uncomfortable.

They are reporting systems, support reporting mechanisms, and educate children about reporting mechanisms on social media platforms and websites. Support Networks create a support network that includes parents, teachers, and trusted adults children can turn to if they encounter inappropriate behavior. Professional Help encourages professional Help, such as counselors or law enforcement, when dealing with serious incidents.

They share real-life examples and case studies to illustrate the dangers and how awareness and education have successfully prevented exploitation. Statistical Data provides statistical data on the prevalence of online predators to highlight the importance of vigilance and education.

Awareness and education are the first lines of defense against online predators. We can create a safer online environment by equipping parents, caregivers, teachers, and children with the knowledge to recognize and respond to predatory behavior. Open communication, ongoing education, and a supportive network are essential in protecting our children from the dangers lurking in the digital world. Together, we can ensure that the internet remains a place of learning and growth, free from the threats posed by online predators.

The threat posed by online child predators is real and significant. By understanding who these predators are and their tactics, we can take proactive steps to protect our children. Education and open communication are our most vital tools in this fight. Please encourage your children to speak openly about their online experiences and monitor their internet use vigilantly.

Together, we can create a safer online environment for our children. Stay informed, stay vigilant, and always prioritize the safety and well-being of our young ones.

A Comprehensive Online Safety Strategy for Children

In today's digital age, children are being exposed to the internet at an increasingly younger age. While offering limitless possibilities for study, creativity, and social interaction, the internet also poses several threats that can jeopardize the safety and well-being of young users. These dangers include cyberbullying, exposure to inappropriate content, online predators, and privacy breaches. Addressing these threats requires a multifaceted strategy involving parents, educators, legislators, and tech corporations. This chapter thoroughly analyzes child internet safety today, highlights important issues, and suggests solutions to mitigate risks and safeguard kids in the digital era.

With the widespread availability of cell phones, tablets, and laptops, children spend more time online than ever. This increased online presence provides children unparalleled access to information and communication opportunities. However, it also exposes them to numerous threats. Cyberbullying, defined as using online communication to harass, threaten, or intimidate others, is a common problem affecting children of all ages. Exposure to inappropriate material such as violence, pornography, and hate speech can also harm children's mental and emotional health. Online predators exploit children's vulnerabilities and innocence, grooming them for sexual exploitation or other types of abuse. Moreover, serious concerns about privacy issues include the unauthorized collection and use of children's data.

Despite growing awareness of these risks, many parents and caregivers must gain the knowledge and skills to supervise and protect their children's online activities effectively. Social media platforms and online services often do not have adequate safeguards to prevent children from accessing harmful content or interacting with potentially dangerous individuals. Balancing children's online autonomy with safety measures is a fundamental challenge in promoting child online safety. While empowering children to explore the digital world and develop digital literacy skills is important, it is equally essential to implement safeguards to protect them from harm.

Another critical challenge is educating children and parents about online risks and safety measures. Many children need to fully understand the potential dangers of the internet, while parents often need more knowledge or resources to monitor and guide their children's online activities effectively. Safeguarding children's online privacy and data security requires strict adherence to laws like the Children's Online Privacy Protection Act (COPPA). However, child safety may only sometimes be prioritized in the design and administration of online platforms, and enforcement measures often need to be strengthened. Holding online platforms accountable for child safety is challenging, as platforms may resist regulatory oversight or be reluctant to implement costly safety measures that could impact their profitability.

Strategies for Protecting Children Online Advising parents to monitor and limit their children's internet use using parental control software can reduce risks. They can effectively safeguard their children by equipping parents with the necessary tools and guidance, including guidelines for internet use and conversation starters on online safety. Integrating digital literacy and online safety education into school curricula can equip students with the knowledge and skills to navigate the digital world safely. Training teachers to recognize signs of online risks and provide support to students experiencing cyberbullying or other forms of online harm is essential.

Strengthening regulations on online platforms to protect children's data and privacy is crucial. Enforcing existing laws such as COPPA and the General Data Protection Regulation (GDPR) more rigorously can

nin

help hold online platforms accountable for safeguarding children's online privacy and security. Developing age-appropriate online platforms and content for children can create safer digital environments. Encouraging child-friendly search engines and browsers that filter out harmful content can help mitigate exposure to inappropriate material.

Encouraging collaboration and understanding among parents, schools, government organizations, and technology businesses is crucial in ensuring children's online safety. Increasing knowledge of recommended practices for online safety through campaigns, seminars, and workshops can enable stakeholders to take preventive action to safeguard children online. Providing counseling services and helplines for children who have experienced online abuse or bullying can offer crucial support. Support groups for parents to share experiences and advice on keeping their children safe online can create a sense of community and solidarity.

If these strategies are implemented and a culture of accountability and vigilance towards child online safety is fostered, children can learn, explore, and interact in a safer digital world. While fostering cross-sector cooperation and collaborative effort is necessary for safeguarding children in the digital age, the welfare of our children is an issue that should be universally supported.

Carly Ryan (January 31, 1992 – February 20, 2007) was an Australian teenager from Stirling, South Australia, who tragically became the first known victim of an online predator in Australia. Her story underscores the dangers of internet relationships and the importance of online safety education.

Carly was a vibrant and creative 15-year-old girl passionate about music and the arts. She enjoyed a close-knit relationship with her family and friends. Like many teenagers of her time, Carly was active on social media and online chat rooms, where she met "Brandon Kane," a persona created by 50-year-old Gary Newman. Newman, posing as a teenage boy, developed a relationship with Carly over an extended period.

Under the guise of "Brandon," Newman manipulated Carly's emotions and gained her trust. In 2007, he traveled from Melbourne to South Australia to meet her. After a brief encounter, Carly discovers the truth about his age and identity. This revelation led to a tumultuous confrontation. Shortly afterward, on February 20, 2007, Newman lured Carly to a secluded beach at Port Elliot, South Australia, where he murdered her.

Carly's death sent shockwaves through the community and highlighted the severe risks associated with online interactions, especially for young and vulnerable individuals. Her mother, Sonya Ryan, became a staunch advocate for online safety, founding the Carly Ryan Foundation in her daughter's memory. The foundation's mission is to promote internet safety education and provide support and resources to young people and their families.

In response to Carly's tragic death, significant legislative changes were made in Australia. In 2017, a decade after her murder, "Carly's Law" was enacted. This law makes it a criminal offense for an adult to misrepresent their age online to a minor with the intent of meeting them in person or committing an offense.

Carly Ryan's story remains a poignant reminder of the potential dangers lurking online and the necessity for vigilance and education to protect young people in the digital age. Her legacy lives on through the work of the Carly Ryan Foundation, which continues to strive for a safer online environment for all children.

By learning from tragedies like Carly's, society can better understand the importance of online safety and work together to protect children from similar fates. The digital age, with all its opportunities, must be navigated with caution, ensuring that the youngest and most vulnerable users are shielded from harm.

The 2009 Plymouth Child Abuse Case

A horrifying example of a child abuse and pedophile network involving at least five persons from different regions of England is the Plymouth child abuse case from 2009. Photographs obtained by Plymouth nursery worker Vanessa George, which showed the mistreatment of up to 64 children, were crucial to the case. This case brought to light the disturbing reality of child molestation by women, with all but one of the ring members being female.

A mother of two, Vanessa George worked at Little Ted's Nursery in Plymouth, an unincorporated not-for-profit association. Between late 2008 and early 2009, George connected with Colin Blanchard and Angela Allen on Facebook. Their communications, initially of a sexual nature, quickly escalated to discussing and committing child abuse. The police later deduced that the trio engaged in a perverse contest to produce the most depraved images. George began taking indecent photographs of children aged two to five at the nursery, as well as a picture of her then 14-year-old daughter. These images were shared with Blanchard, who, in turn, shared them with Allen.

Tracy Lyons, a mother of nine from Portsmouth, Hampshire, was also in the ring. Lyons entered a guilty plea in March 2010 to several offenses, which included inducing a kid under the age of 13 to engage in sexual behavior, assaulting a child by penetration, and disseminating obscene pictures of minors.

A fifth member, Tracy Dawber, a care worker from Southport, Merseyside, was implicated after a colleague of Colin Blanchard discovered images of sexual abuse on Blanchard's laptop while he was abroad. This discovery was reported to Greater Manchester Police, leading to Blanchard's arrest upon his return to England. The investigation uncovered indecent images on his computer, along with incriminating emails and text messages between Blanchard, George, and Allen.

On the evening of June 8, police arrested George at Little Ted's Nursery. She was brought to court on June 11, facing charges of sexual assault and making, possessing, and distributing indecent images of children. George admitted to creating 124 indecent images, specifically targeting young children at the nursery. The absence of identifiable faces in these images made it challenging for police to identify the victims.

The trial was presided over by Mr. Justice Royce. George entered a guilty plea to six charges of creating and disseminating offensive images of minors as well as seven counts of sexual assault. She was given an indeterminate sentence on December 15, 2009, with a minimum period of seven years, subject to her demonstrating that she presented no future harm to society.

Angela Allen also pleaded guilty to distributing indecent images and four counts of sexual assault involving children. She was given an indeterminate sentence with a minimum tariff of five years on the same day as George.

Blanchard was given an indeterminate sentence with a minimum period of nine years on January 10, 2011. Tracy Lyons received a seven-year term, while Tracy Dawber received a four-year sentence. Child safety activists were outraged when Lyons was freed from jail in October 2011, nine months after her conviction. Kidscape's Claude Knights denounced her early release, calling it a betrayal of the families and victims.

This case significantly increased awareness of female pedophiles and the scope of their offenses. It challenged the stereotype that only men sexually abuse children and highlighted that female offenders often act independently for their gratification. Michele Elliott of Kidscape emphasized the necessity of recognizing that women do abuse children, sometimes without male coercion, for the sake of the victims.

The case led Plymouth City Council to launch a serious case review, published on November 4, 2010. The review concluded that while George was ultimately responsible, several failings in the nursery's management and procedures had created an environment conducive to her abuse. It criticized a 2008 Ofsted inspection for rating the nursery "good" in child protection, suggesting the framework for such inspections might be inadequate.

Little Ted's Nursery, located on Laira Green Primary School grounds, closed following the initial arrests in June 2009. In September 2010, a new facility, Greenshoots preschool unit, opened in its place. This new unit was jointly managed with

The Franklin Murder, Satanism, and Child Abuse Cover-Up

"The Franklin Cover-up and Child Abuse, Satanism, and Murder" is a highly controversial and disturbing case that gained notoriety in the late 1980s and early 1990s. It revolves around allegations of widespread child sexual abuse, satanic rituals, and even murder, with purported ties to high-ranking officials and influential figures.

The case originated in Omaha, Nebraska, where allegations of child abuse and exploitation first surfaced. It involved the Franklin Community Federal Credit Union, which was accused of being a front for a pedophile ring that preyed on vulnerable children. As investigations unfolded, shocking testimonies emerged, detailing instances of sexual abuse, torture, and even claims of human sacrifice.

One of the key figures in the case was Lawrence King Jr., a prominent businessman and political figure who was implicated as a central figure in the alleged pedophile ring. King's lavish lifestyle and connections to influential individuals fueled speculation about a cover-up orchestrated to protect him and other influential figures involved.

However, despite numerous testimonies and evidence presented by victims and witnesses, the case was plagued by controversy, inconsistencies, and allegations of intimidation and suppression. Some critics dismissed the allegations as unfounded conspiracy theories, while others argued that there were significant gaps in the investigation and prosecution of those involved.

The Franklin Cover-up case continues to be a subject of debate and speculation, with proponents of the allegations claiming that it exposes deep-seated corruption and depravity within powerful institutions. However, skeptics caution against jumping to conclusions without concrete evidence and emphasize the importance of thorough and unbiased investigations into allegations of child abuse and exploitation.

David and I heard about this case many years ago in Masonic circles, where whispers of dark secrets and hidden agendas circulated. The case has since become a focal point for those questioning the integrity of institutions and the lengths to which some may go to protect their interests, even at the expense of innocent lives.

DeCamp wrote of an interview he had with Paul Bonacci, one of the child victims of Larry King. What Bonacci knew, if valid, could damage many important people. He had been abducted and used, sexually abused, and tortured since he was kidnapped. He thought it was his duty to fight back and possibly save other children from being used. On March 25, 1999, Paul Bonacci won his civil case in the U.S. District Court in Lincoln, Nebraska, where the judge awarded him $1,000,000 in compensatory damages and ruled that threatening or harassing Paul Bonacci, Lawrence E. King, who was then in prison, "proved the most devastating form of harassment.

The Franklin Cover-Up: Child Abuse, Satanism, and Murder in Nebraska is a book written by John DeCamp over nine years starting in 1988. It tells the story of a government and a state in Nebraska that were involved in a child abuse ring. The book has a preface by William Colby, the former director of the CIA, and is dedicated to Gary Caradori, a Nebraska state investigator, and William Colby, who died mysteriously. DeCamp was a former senator in the Nebraska State Senate and was a lawyer in Lincoln, Nebraska. He represented a victim of the pedophile ring, Alisha Owen, and after she had been convicted of perjury in court, he worked on her appeal.

Therefore, The Franklin case has nothing to do with financial scandals, not with Father Franklin, who supported Caesar, papal bulls, and the Jesuit Inquisition! Incidentally, a pizzeria in Washington called Franklin Square is located near Saint John's Church and Saint John's

Rectory (1619-2007). Good to know, right? To end this story: If the objective of the revival of Franklin Case is to simplify the uncertainty of Prince George's murderer, we would like to report two helpful tips. The Washington Times report remembers that "Maj. Gen. John K. Singlaub, former head of the "6th Army " base, "Southern Command," and "John Birch Society," can say everything he knows. Highly unlikely, given that a future "Taylor of TI" organization advocates the "anti-Semitic" "Protocols of the Wise Men of" "Sion" and the National Veterans' Organization of America (NOVA) enjoyed representing itself as the organization that sponsored the "race" for a while, mainly because it could serve as a reliable address for the worst prejudices of the Military Religious Freedom Foundation!

The Franklin Cover-Up and Child Abuse, Satanism, and Murder in Nebraska, by John W. DeCamp, is a descendant of mysteries from the 1980s that promised to sell big in the book market. The original stories were narrated in the 1980s by patients and physicians at Dr. King's Clinic for Atomic Veterans, which existed in Galveston, Texas. They were also reported in major newspapers such as the Washington Times and small publications such as Common Sense in Illinois, the Idaho Observer, and the Veteran. There were four problems. However, the entire North American press never corroborated the news, the alleged crimes vanished from the earth, the only person on death row who could accuse the people mentioned by the papers during his judgment was Geraldo Rivera, and above all, Mr. DeCamp refused to call for an investigation of the CIA, which he allegedly belonged to. For those who love mysteries. And you'll have to wait for the sequel when Richard Nixon will appear posthumously as the head of a cult in NebrState.

Besides Larry King, the recent witnesses fingered other well-known adults to the news media. The most notable of these people was the senior man in the Nebraska delegation to the U.S. Senate, the highest-ranking Republican member of the Senate Agriculture Committee. Both houses of the Nebraska State Legislature are Republican, as are four of the six congressional seats that Nebraska is allocated. The Nebraska delegation was also the most conservative member of the U.S. Congress in terms of the leading role they played in the movement to deny federal job opportunities to any citizen who indulged in non-violent sexual behavior with another adult. With so many Nebraska citizens entrusting our lawmakers' families to their favorite babysitters, Andersen's disclosures have also created the deep concern of taking the manure out of next week's Omaha mayoral election.

The Franklin Scandal stayed a dirty little secret until January of this year when Mark Andersen of the Omaha World-Herald published a story of the previous week's federal grand jury testimony of two young men who had helped Army and Senate figure Larry King sexually exploit young boys. Andersen wasted no time telling readers that "the story is a twisted tale of kids, drugs, and money." The United States Attorney for the District of Nebraska had recently called federal law enforcement officials in for a working meeting and pledged, "I want you to know that I don't care where this investigation leads. If it fits, we are going to go with it." It's nice to know that some U.S. authorities are not subject to pressures from superiors in high places.

The Omaha Franklin investigation did start with a sexual focus. Boys appeared to have been transported to Washington, D.C., and New York to perform sexual favors to influence the votes of high-level politicians. Such trips were allegedly arranged from within the Franklin Credit Union by its vindictive and prominent manager, involving McMartin graduate Lawrence E. King. Local homosexual prostitution involvement initially surfaced when Omaha Police personnel named this form of abuse during the Seattle investigation that resulted in the U.S. Post Office suspending "Boy's Town" mailing privileges. Sister Morality's enveloping standard protection of hometown predilections for this activity was possibly Gary Caradori's second case of damaged integrity. The "King of Boys Town" tried to avoid arrest for questioning by stating that his life was in danger on a national media outlet. Caradori then noted that no one would believe that a Director of the juvenile facility and an attorney would be involved in such activities, ignoring that a nationally prominent columnist in the State was following this line of investigation. The FBI and the Post Office declined to follow up, leaving last-minute evidence that died with Caradori in a plane crash. The same factors could have influenced the FBI's current handling of an investigation by John

DeCamp, State Senator, beginning six months after the repeal of the Omaha Prostitution Ordinance.

The initial thrust in the investigation of the Franklin, Nebraska exposure came from prosecution witnesses and concerned the alleged physical abuse of children. This writer became involved in the case as a Christian minister. My purpose in writing this report is to reveal to the church and community some of the spiritual and even Satanic implications of the Franklin Scandal. Moral issues and court evidence should be held higher before those claiming the name of Christ can provide spiritually responsible reactions to the events described herein. The covering up of the true nature of the Franklin investigation goes hand in hand with the protection of the perpetrators, the drug/homosexual network, and the Swat Team killers. Such calls follow precisely the design of Satan in falsely accusing the innocent while protecting the real child abusers. It's time to shift the violated children and their sexually abusive perpetrators from the public agenda of Walter Mondale, the Justice Department, and Gary Caradori's so-called law enforcement brethren into "the hands of an angry God."

Abstract: A thorough investigation into the widespread child sexual abuse and the parallel of powerful but hidden alleged child sex rings of influential people in the U.S. capital has been blunted in many ways by societal disbelief, inherent institutional conflicts of interest, the magnitude of the investigation, and by the presence in the backing of broad forces of many elements — some of which fight the investigative inquiry. Numbered examples illustrate how part of the broad forces associated with the politics of societal dispute settlement becomes part of such an officially bedimmed situation. The presented matter suggests the need for broad-ranging and well-resourced research by law and social scientists that ideally is outside any control of conducting public government entities.

Due to time constraints, one request was received for a copy of this 4. Investigations and Cover-up. Both records were sent to her by mail. Next time I speak with her, I will learn more about what's going on in this area, and I would appreciate receiving any information on this general subject.

In the 12 days since federal and State law enforcement agencies swooped down on the farm, they have interviewed more than 50 children and taken statements from more than 75 witnesses. An investigation by FBI agents, noting the presence of large amounts of drugs and alcohol and the fact that in some children, incest was reported by non-related caretakers, assumed that the parents were heavily involved. Each child who is determined to have been sexually abused is placed in foster care and cannot have contact with their family unless the child's relatives are cleared to be among the non-abusers. All non-abusing relatives are being encouraged to seek legal custody of the child if feasible. All children are being debriefed about their family members, and all adults are fingerprinted to determine if previous charges involving other children are suspected to be connected.

On June 21, 1988, nearly 40 police officers searched the Washington FBI officials for evidence on an 800-acre spread in rural southern Douglas County believed to contain clandestine grave sites related to the State. It is located 13 miles south of the spot where the body of a 12-year-old Twin Cities girl was found on March 25. Authorities believe that a large ring of child molesters, abusing boys and girls as young as three, participated and was using the farm. Law enforcement officials in five states have been investigating the abuse ring since the body of the girl was discovered in a field off Minnesota 29 near Alexandria. The investigation has led to the filing of criminal charges against four men, two of whom are in jail.

The Franklin file has a rich history of difficulty in the public discussion and investigation relating to the matter of the sexual exploitation of children. We have seen a few accusations made to others, such as the King materials; however, in the following few chapters, we have the stories of the kitchen cabinet and the people who were living their lives. It is essential to see where they are distributing these criminal matters. "Disinformation," it can be seen, is a two-edged sword. Now, the arrow can be revealed. Some of these big shots are snuffing children as parties for the big shots in the White House contained child pornography. How about those sexual predation charges?

With the merging of findings in various investigations, the story of a criminal enterprise centered in New York, Washington, and seemingly Omaha has emerged. Money, drugs, party favors for the wealthy and connected, children for sex, and at the end of the line, children for sacrifice. It is a complex story, but by dying, Alisha Owen rendered one tremendous service to her fellow citizens. By willing her deposition, she has provided corroboration that sex parties with children were organized for the big shots in Washington, D.C., which were then not disclosed to any authorities. And now the Franklin story makes one more giant step. With corroboration between the Franklin evidence and statements in the Danny King matter, evidence has emerged relating to Satanism.

The Nebraska situation is further complicated by the fact that the legislature there has taken the phenomenon of satanic ritual abuse seriously enough not only to hear testimony on the subject but also to pass two laws specifically designed to deal with it. One created a task force to study the substantiated incidence of ritual abuse of children, to gather and disseminate information, and to recommend state policy and legislation. Investigations were not to be limited to criminal behavior or imprisonment of the abusers. The goal was to "compile information, provide assistance and support the healing process of children who have been subjected to ritual abuse; and to marshal support for federal and state law enforcement agencies, private organizations and agencies that provide for follow-up treatment of victims of ritual abuse." These laws, passed only last year (1988), were introduced after the Franklin Credit Union collapse and were heavily supported by the senator deposed in the Franklin affair. They may be the result of genuine legislative concern, or they may be designed to encourage belief in the Franklin allegations by members of the public, so the public might make the same mistake the legislature did and find out too late that the evidence had not lived up to the rhetoric.

Larry King remains a "penthouse prisoner" in jail. He still uses drugs, takes teenage prisoners on unsupervised trips in a private Lear jet, and is allowed to go out at night allegedly to serve pizza to friends and return them to the jail. Why, after all the horror stories have come out in hundreds of publications worldwide, has he not been released on $500,000 bail? "The initial motion to set bail was reported to be denied by order of Judge Warwick." Was this Bill Warwick?

The fallout for many of those involved in the Franklin Cover-Up was swift and severe. The State's NationStates was forced to abdicate his throne after Anthony Ridder, president of Knight-Ridder, owner of the newspaper chain, put a reporter on the story. More than 100 criminal convictions were found to be based on perjured testimony, and Nebraska's conservative Unicameral of 49 legislators, of which 6 are members of a "Reaganite" think tank, abolished the House-Senate Franklin investigative committee, fearing it would open up a floodgate of appeals.

American society should take notice of the story, double our efforts, and pour funds into aftercare and protection for sexually abused children, for they are our future. It would be a tribute to the battered and brutalized survivors of the Omaha scandal if the exposure of those who arrogantly believe they are untouchable would hasten a public concern about child abuse. In conclusion, I hope the Franklin incident will be remembered not for the perpetrators' sake but as a poignant reminder that whatever the obstacles, children are our future and must be served. The obscenity of any cover-up or any conspiracy is that they threaten more extensive harm to more children.

The Nebraska "Franklin" chapter relates to other recent political scandals indicating an alarming abuse of power, although few have equaled the Franklin scandal in the misuse of power and authority. The "Franklin" story still has the potential to become the scandal of the century with eventual hearings and potential exposure for "America's darkest hour." The victims affected by the "Franklin" case will always pay the ultimate price. Unfortunately, their lives exemplify the spirit of what President Lyndon B. Johnson called "the greediest city of all."

Investigating the Link Between the Atlanta Child Murders and Child Trafficking

My memories of the Atlanta Child Murders are etched in my mind from a young age, a dark shadow looming over my childhood. Growing up, the haunting stories of innocent lives lost and a city gripped by fear left an indelible mark on my psyche. Yet, it wasn't until about twenty years ago that David and I found ourselves unexpectedly drawn back into the chilling realm of this infamous case.

It was a seemingly ordinary evening in Atlanta, where the glitz and glamor of an upscale house party starkly contrasted the grim realities lurking just beyond the city's bright lights. Amidst the chatter and laughter of the guests, whispers of the Atlanta Child Murders began to circulate, stirring memories long buried beneath the surface of my consciousness.

As David and I listened to the murmurs of intrigue and speculation, a sense of curiosity and determination ignited. With a shared desire to uncover the truth behind the dark veil of mystery, we embarked on a journey that would lead us down a path fraught with danger and uncertainty.

Soon after our initial inquiries, we found ourselves approached by representatives from a local university and a group of psychics who sought our assistance in delving deeper into the mysteries surrounding the Atlanta Child Murders. Eager to shine a light on the shadowy secrets that had haunted Atlanta for decades, we agreed to lend our expertise to the investigation.

However, our collaboration was short-lived, marred by threats and intimidation that forced our university partners and the psychics to withdraw from the endeavor. Despite the dangers that lurked in the shadows, David and I refused to be deterred, continuing our research independently with a steadfast resolve to uncover the truth.

In this chapter, we invite you to join us on a journey into the heart of darkness as we explore the chilling connections between the Atlanta Child Murders and the sinister forces that lie beneath the surface of society. Together, we will confront uncomfortable truths, expose hidden atrocities, and honor the memory of those whose lives were tragically cut short by unspeakable evil.

Atlanta's Hartsfield Airport is one of the most frequently utilized child trafficking portals in the country – and the world. The high incidence of missing/murdered and troubled foster children in downtown Atlanta does indicate specific problems in the placement of state and other children in the area. This was reiterated in the Atlanta public hearing on foster care in the early 1990s. Among the most challenging problems for foster children who were sexually and ritually abused was the disbelief and neglect by any available adult advocates – at least until the foster child's finders arrived – who then delivered the foster child back over to officially appointed (and questionably reliable) clandestine interfamily pedophile networks. These child abuse/pornographic networks often get their foster children from their own specifically arranged foster care adoptions somehow.

This paper discusses the connection between the Atlanta Cases of the Missing and Murdered Children (1979-1981) – in which at least 28 children up to the age of 21 were either missing and never found, kidnapped and found murdered, or discovered as a floater – and worldwide child trafficking, especially in reception and transit centers and at major airports; as well as in child sex trafficking and both historical child abductions and in the snuff movie trade – as well as in Ritual Abuse, including the interconnection in the new revelations coming forth, that claim that they were part of major political, military, and banking/drug/currency fraud scandals. Little concrete research exists at this time regarding the veracity of these claims; this paper calls for future research on the area.

The investigation took place from 1979 to 1981 and included the deaths of 28 African American children and young adults. These deaths occurred during 22 months from 1979 to 1981. Many of those deaths were the results of shootings, and others were directly related to the nature of the 29 bridges that run through the Atlanta metropolitan area. Since the murders were concentrated in a specific location, many working theories could have resulted in an end to these hideous acts. Children are abducted many times a day. Some are taken by unauthorized fathers who are fighting for custody of their children. It is common for many of these cases to be easily forgotten by those around us as we try to lead our busy and mundane lives. A fascinating aspect of the criminal justice system's handling of child kidnappings is whose kidnapping cases are deemed newsworthy. The late 1990s and early 2000s show a trend of fathers and mothers receiving similar punishments for the abduction of their children. With a spotlight on one of the most dangerous custody battles in recent history, the public was led to believe that Ellanna Harris's mother may have been connected to the Atlanta Child Murders.

The Atlanta Child Murders occurred in Atlanta, Georgia, from 1979 to 1981. Atlanta was in a time of increased adult fears about the welfare of children in general. Across the country, campaigns began to inform adults about the presence of sexual predators and teach children how to avoid or confront attempted abductions. During this time, the milk carton campaign to place pictures of missing children on containers became commonplace. Campaigns focused on the distribution of materials to better understand sexual predators. Increased outrage led to the ability to get policies related to sexual abuse implemented. Prosecutor guidelines, children's statutes of limitation for sexual abuse, and relaxed hearsay evidence rules were all approved as a result of the Denver and Atlanta child murders.

The United States Department of Education (DOE) receives $58 billion in funding. They are specifically in charge of handling the money that goes to the public school system. This is a significant portion of their responsibility. The DOE oversees the attainment of the needs of 14,000 school districts in America. Imagine the large volume of paperwork necessary to track all these children. The DOJ helps the DOE. The Department of Justice has gone to great lengths to assist the Doe by attempting to organize theirs and the necessary research "into a database which case" would be the linkage descendants of children kidnapped and abused through the money that is allocated from the government. Why should we be concerned with such an insignificant aspect of the Office of Management and Budget?

At present, there are notifying missing children in the United States. This does not mean the other 841,183 children have been kidnapped, abducted, trafficked for forced labor/sex, etc. They and their families may be in worse danger. With black market adoption fees climbing to upwards of $250,000, it is possible that the missing children have dropped off the database because they have been willingly stolen. Children are worth a lot of money. What is the value to these children? Once the innocence of a child has been stolen, they are worth whatever they can be utilized for. From snuff films to white slavery to being sold as enslaved people, part business business is booming. In 1986, postal workers and police agencies handling kidnappings received over 2,000 inquiries each week about runaways from potential kidnapping victims from people who take care of most of this day today, the nation's largest second class," the second largest in the country. The first largest is United Parcel Service, which also delivers missing children! Shall we now handle them with equal care and urgency?

Although the forms of child exploitation look diverse, the essential feature of this phenomenon lies in the fact that it is the activities of profit-making organizations denying children the chance to exercise their right to receive support and respect, which is usually provided to them in society. Child trafficking is similar to organized crime both in some procedures and the object of the offense.

And now, the solution that would be provided corresponds with such a scheme. Another dimension is associated with the fact that the term' child trafficking' in part should not be divided from the term' immigration.' Such a circumstance does not become an obstacle to seeking preventive measures to protect victims and provide punishment for violators. On the contrary, the fact that it is associated with other problems should give an advantage in searching for solutions, and the mere existence of its association with other issues should not become a reason for denying it the status of an independent problem.

From slavery to child exploitation, the European Union's conquest of the best ways to control child trafficking, the European Court of Human Rights has accepted that spanking should be a joint right. At that, the problem of slavery of a general character would be less, and the issue of child exploitation is more accentuated.

The problem of child trafficking has existed for a long time, although in different historical periods and countries, it would be differently named. The modern term' child trafficking' is characterized by the fact that it includes violation of two prominent human rights, which are the main feature of the international legal basis. These are the right to live (in one's community) and the right to be free from violence, torture, or inhuman punishment. Besides, the term 'trafficking' covers the legal basis of inhuman trade, similar to the modern definition.

The lack of verifiable evidence, aside from a smattering of high-profile cases that showed no link to snuff films or reports of hoax videos that purportedly depicted actual killings (which had shown to be scenes from foreign horror and pornographic movies), and definition problem – particularly that of a meritless discussion regarding the qualification of snuff films, i.e. whether the film must contain the entire filmed act or simply the death portion that allegedly satisfied the clients – tended to replace the reports with unfounded stories, speculation, and false claims made about real-life snuff films. However, despite this lack of authentic evidence to prove the existence of a bona fide snuff film industry, snuff films remained in the public's collective consciousness as an enigmatic, cryptic topic.

Snuff films: Understanding the phenomenon. In terms of popular understanding, snuff films, also known as "true death videos," are generally viewed as potentially involving the recording of heinous acts such as the murders of individuals via various means and the subsequent sale of the videos to individuals who derive pleasure from such killings. Most of the confusion regarding snuff films, particularly its use as a term, stems from the actual context of snuff films themselves. Reports of "true death" videos first emerged in the late 1960s as rumors from South America, allegations of films that derived pleasure from, essentially, the pre-recorded violent torture, sexual exploitation, and eventual murder of a woman or young girl, sold directly to private (and elite) clientele.

"Viewers" (sometimes thought to be "observers") in even some "legitimate" don't care too much or are sometimes utterly indifferent to the overall treatment and quality of these "snuff-like" films. They believe that these tapes' "lower-end production values" can be bypassed because the content easily satisfies a consumer's morbid curiosity.

Scrolling through available literature and discussions on the topic reveals that military shootouts, police chases, private violent confrontations, and, most importantly, prison executions are "checkable and verifiable" examples of "snuff-like" films, considering the injuries and deaths that have occurred to realistic and current individuals. In the past few years, international letters involving inquiries from collectors have been directed to prisoner advocate and writer Stephen Donaldson. These letters ask about the specifics of certain situations in which prisoners are executed, hoping their corresponding incidents will be accurately depicted in whatever film is requested.

Today, information that defines and describes snuff films can be found in film journals. However, upon examination of the subject's history, there appears to be no concrete evidence or proof from sources, such as film journals, which define the true essence of snuff films. This absence of substantive documentation allows the creation of myths and legends to evolve. Some argue that "snuff-like" films exist; such films are considered collector's items, "homemade tapes of actual occurrences" that feature deaths caught on film.

In 1978, snuff films were shown to merely be a myth by Alan Petridis of the U.S. Attorney's Special Prosecution Division and the FBI during a seminar held at Quantico. Petridis based his evidence on his readings of court files. Specifically, one case was described at the workshop, which involved the methadone poisoning of a 5-year-old girl from the Albany,

New York area. Petridis stated that there was no concrete proof that snuff films exist but assured his students that he had heard reports claiming that snuff films were linked to illegal drug dealings and the Colombian mafia.

Snuff films, by definition, are commercially available films that record the death of a person at another person's hands for the viewer's sexual arousal. According to author Brotman, the term "snuff" is believed to have been coined during the late 1970s; however, the actual death of victims has been filmed for entertainment for many years before this term was created. Since their recognition, snuff films have often been labeled as cinematic legends instead of documentaries.

Sexual abuse in childhood fractures the lives of veteran men and women, often leaving broken adults, loveless marriages, and dead and deprived children in its wake. There is also evidence that child sexual abuse destroys the lives of some older adolescents, particularly if the abuse is prolonged, sadistic, and involves multiple offenders or if the individual child has a close relationship with the offender. The magnitude of the problems that result from the sexual abuse of children suggests that child sex abusers are committing severe, violent, assaultive crimes against their child victims. This study will look at the implications of a connection between the child murder cases labeled the Atlanta Child Murders and child traffickers. The cases that were modeled for the creation of AMBER Alert were driven by economic forces, the obscene profits to be made in the wholesale of children from the home and parents, from whom doctors kidnap them, from where they are shipped and handed off to pimps and traffickers, and then are relabeled as slave prostitutes starring as child porno actors in snuff films. The abductors, black market baby sellers, child traffickers, and child murder for-profit enterprises exploit children. It is appropriate that we look back and remember the modern-day child traffickers known as the Atlanta Child Murderer.

The sexual abuse of children: prevalence and impact. The sexual abuse of children is a significant problem in the United States. Approximately 1 in 5 girls and 1 in 20 boys are sexually abused by the age of 18. In the overwhelming majority of these cases, the abuser is a family member or someone known to the child. The vast majority of sexual abuse of children goes unreported and is a well-kept family secret. Up to 40% of victims never tell anyone. Only 10-20% of those children who are sexually abused are abused by someone unknown to them. Child sexual abuse has been linked to several psychological, emotional, and physical effects, including depression, PTSD, anxiety, promiscuity, and increased chances of an adult partner murdering them.

First, molestation covers touching the child's genital area over or under clothing, indecent exposure or exhibitionism, and exposing the child to sexual content through models, books, or photos, while it does not include assault. The exact definition applies to all other forms, except sodomy, intercourse, and exhibitionism, and rape of a male involves fellatio. In boys, molestation turns to pedophilia when an adult initiates the action. The exact definition applies to all other forms except sodomy, anal, oral, and sexual intercourse. In the judgment of the public, female child sexual abuse is less than male child sexual abuse.

We can define child sexual abuse as a pervasive problem affecting millions of American women today. Based on the percentages above, it is clear that the majority of quizzed males and females in the United States were, in fact, either victims of child sexual abuse or knew of someone in their family who was a victim. In Table 1, the breakdown shows the rates of child sexual abuse of quizzed members within families in the United States during 1978-1981. Hidden in families in each category, such as females, males, and both, the percentages are very alarming when totaled. Before I continue with these statistics, which indicate a problem that is not easily diagnosed and dealt with in families, I would like to give you what child sexual abuse is. Child sexual abuse, which includes molestation, incest, rape, boys, and all forms, is increasingly devastating.

Like many serial killer cases, the question of trafficking, snuff films, or pornography does not cross the minds of investigators conducting major murder investigations. Case managers and investigators are primarily concerned with identifying suspects to appease society's pressures and are not worried about what might have created the monster in the first place. The families and the community are very rarely interviewed about potential kidnappings their family member might have experienced before getting murdered and disposed of in the crime scene area, nor do the case agents follow up on possible clues or witnesses detailing specifics of the case before it was taken out of the children killing category and before Williams became the scapegoat. Little snippets of missing information are dismissed as trivial and not connected to the case.

The Atlanta Child Murders consisted of the killings of 28 children, adolescents, and adults in Atlanta, Georgia, between the ages of 9 and 28 from 1979 to 1981. Wayne Williams became the scapegoat and was heavily convicted of committing the murders and was sentenced to life in prison to avoid a second trial. After the trial, the case was considered officially closed as Williams laughed during the case hearing and had reportedly been linked to at least 20 more murders in the area. Still, the case was quickly dropped due to lack of evidence. There was never a proper investigation conducted on possible child trafficking, snuff films, or pornography. Instead, the case was framed to ensnare Williams as the only suspect responsible for the Atlanta killings.

The reports of a person attempting to entice a child to approach his car began in July of 1979. By September of 1980, the situation had escalated so much that the police were staking out public areas. However, the homicide division was not interested in an accused murderer due to jurisdiction. Their exclusivity ended in July of 1980. The obligation to solve twenty-seven murders is enough to motivate anyone: the politicians, parents, and other citizens wanted a resolution. The high-profile nature of the murders was causing significant problems for the city and the state of Georgia. What was originally jurisdictional became personal and professional."

"Much research on the "Atlanta Child Murders" has excluded information related to the connections to snuff films, child trafficking, and sexual abuse. This study seeks to comprehend why such connections are seldom discussed. A primary reason is that without some context, those connections are merely improbable elements in a story about a heinous criminal. It is necessary to offer background information to orient the reader to why this particular crime might encompass child trafficking, snuff films, and sexual abuse. This section provides a condensed version of the events, from the police stopping a man due to a possible linkage to child abduction cases to the capture of the only individual who could have committed all the murders.

An Analysis of Jessie Marie Czebotar's Testimony

Czebotar views saviors as the only potential remedy and sees the reason for and the primary danger of these programs as extraterrestrial A.I. Furthermore. At the same time, she interviews these people under challenging states of being; she stresses their desirability as members of elite members of society who have withstood dislocation from what she tentatively calls a star matrix 17 paradigms as physical beings. This framing bucks conspiracy theories about a global reset as the control system's effort not be excluded from a higher paradigm. Czebotar ties the star paradigm back to Bible days and Jesus. Like Jenny Hill and painted C.I.A. wife Brice Taylor before her, she describes a special message about Jesus being consistently relayed during these assaults. Let us not impose our personal theologies on her analysis nor read her acceptance of such messages uncritically. If she is deprogramming mind-controlled individuals emerging with knowledge of this victim narrative, religious saviorism is likely to come through as part of their reality frames. Therefore, her perception is firmly pro-saviors and intensely colored with divine narrative elements.

Jessie Marie Czebotar is a former MKUltra programmer who is now deprogramming former program participants as well as pulling information from Alpha and Beta level individuals who she considers victims bred and conditioned by a more sophisticated, technological interface as more pliable than the earlier groups. Her program activity was so robust and complex that some participants worked for multigenerational programs, with some having significant authority and range within the organizations. Her technology has been withdrawn since she has become vocal and credible on public platforms. The narrative and functional attributes of Alpha, Beta, Delta, Omega, and Theta model programming were exposed on YouTube. This work further exposes symbols, branding, and even more detail about these most desperately needed human beings.

Jessie Marie Czebotar is stating a lot of valuable information about the Illuminati. What she is not entirely open about is the level of mind control programming and the multiple personality layers that have been placed within her by the same Illuminati that she stated in her deposition that she wanted to be removed from. Her constant reference to God is again hiding the facade of the Illuminati, which is an organization owned and operated at the very top by hostile extraterrestrials. The Illuminati plan to destroy our ability to do anything without permission, including being able to access critical thought that would be critical of the Illuminati. By having a separate controlling personality referred to as a higher self in place, the Illuminati believe that they are one step closer to having ultimate control over humanity. The book The Illuminati Formula to Create an Undetectable Total Mind Control enslaved person by Fritz Springmeier and Cisco Wheeler gives a step-by-step guide on how these multiple personalities are manufactured, the reasons for creating them, and documentation of actual documents and memos that the F.B.I. confiscated at the turn of the millennium.

I recently spent three hours listening to a video where Jessie Marie Czebotar speaks to Pastor Scott A. Johnson on the YouTube channel Believer's Victory Fellowship. Further down below are some personal thoughts about Jessie Marie Czebotar and her information. Jessie is telling the truth; I believe she was an Illuminati member. However, there are some questionable aspects of who is sharing her story. What I would say to Jessie is that the Illuminati created Christianity. Therefore, a person who truly wants to divest themself from the Illuminati completely must also reject Christianity. The information I will share below divulges details from her testimony to showcase the areas where she is correct and incorrect. I am not trying to blemish her character. This was a very useful assemblage of information.

Czebotar presents the Illuminati and satanic cults as highly organized institutions that have existed for thousands of years. The bloodlines of the ancient era have expanded and become de facto leaders in the modern corporatocracy, some establishing themselves as family names in industries that currently dominate the public domain. The Illuminati family is proposed as being an electro-technological priesthood. Their power structure includes only the top 300-500 corporations worldwide, and they can access a defense budget double what the U.S. government determines. Within the power hierarchy, the facilitator priests are responsible for distributing knowledge down to the members. Corporate leaders of the family are termed the C.E.O.s. They handle the financial and economic assets and marketing strategies and direct the overall influence on the public. On another level, bishops are responsible for geopolitical and military strategy. Finally, there are "advocates" or "dabblers" who are not part of the Illuminati but "dabble" or help carry out their work.

While Jessie's vast and in-depth experiences with the Illuminati can never be refuted, several critical themes emerge for investigation through an analysis of the testimony. This section of the paper covers these themes, which are offered for consideration in studying the Czebotar case and its implications.

Czebotar describes herself as a spiritual healer who uses the foundational energy of Almighty God to work to help bring balance to the collective. She would be, at first glance, the last possible person to embrace what some would describe as occult or satanic viewpoints.

Nonetheless, Czebotar relays a remarkable narrative about her alleged parentage from a family practicing black magic in part related to the employment of high-ranking positions in U.S. banks to ensure she could find a person willing to carry the "Satan entity" and regain access to her soul. The description is essentially of possible alternate personality and other dissociative symptoms of complex PTSD rather than the alien or reptilian experiences that are generally depicted as core conspiratorial theories.

On August 24, 2019, Jessie Marie Czebotar presented on spirituality and her work as a spiritual healer. She described her experiences in Christian spiritual healing, as well as the deep research she claims she has conducted into Satanism and secret societies. Czebotar's description of what many scientists might consider as fringe, divergent, conspiratorial, or possibly baseless ideas are essential to discuss here from a Science, Technology, and Human Values perspective, not because Czebotar's thoughts come from far-outlying realms, but because these testimonies have embraced theories long present in American spiritualist subcultures. An academic political science perspective provides a further, deep consideration, asking inherently materialistic questions.

It is also necessary to prevent the core of Czebotar's testimony from being used for someone's wrongful or mischievous purpose to cause damage to those who have nothing to do with the crimes. Those who are indeed victims of the crimes and those who are merely accused of the crimes are in the wrong category at present. Still, only the genuine truth that would support independent legal proceedings could correctly classify them. Given the above, the masked person maintaining and trafficking to whom Czebotar testified so far was in Australia because the essential links between these people and Czebotar have not been revealed. Such evidence, presented as a whole but not in legal proceedings, may significantly impact many individuals and their privacy.

One question from this research is the reliability of Czebotar's testimony. In all countries that adhere to the principles of the rule of law and criminal law, the guilt of a charged person can be based solely on the results of fair, thorough, and diligent criminal proceedings in which evidence was examined to determine the facts. Her testimony has considerable power regardless of whether Czebotar is telling the truth. This ability should be used for good purposes, and the core of her testimony should be verified in fair, transparent, and fully independent legal proceedings. This would satisfy the above criteria and thus support the rule of law and the Andrew Neather English state, which operates on the presumption of innocence of any charged person until their guilt has been confirmed by the results of proceedings conducted in their presence.

Czebotar says in the interview with Matias De Stefano at approx. 8'

59" that such fantasy traumatic programming can be recognized because, for such a child, too many bad things happened for real to them. We shall look at two child victims, one in the past and the other in the present, who have been listed as fantasy-inclined by the alternative media to cover up the wrongs done to them. These cases, which have been in the public arena for many years, are those of Joan of Arc in the 15th century and of Alisa and Gabriel Dearman in the 21st century, mostly in 2014 and 2015. The cases are remarkable in their similarities, the ages of the perpetrators, and the lengths to which some went to try to suppress the truth about the young minds involved in the cases.

In my opinion, one of the most vital points of Czebotar's testimony is that other sources can corroborate it, and indeed, some parts of her testimony were known by some before Czebotar made it public. We shall look at the corroboration of her testimony in section 3.1. through 3.7., reserving some specific topics for later sections. One of the significant traits of Satanic mind control of youth and children, according to Czebotar, is that the children are encouraged to present some of the "memories" from their abuse as imaginative fantasies of no real significance. The purpose of this is to prevent the children from knowing that they are being severely traumatized and fragmented for purposes of control, to prevent them from receiving validation that they were indeed put through such experiences, and also to allow abusers to dismiss any testimony given by the children as "just imagination."

Claims that influential people are involved in incredibly heinous behavior without any evidence are unfair, potentially ruinous, and enable autocratic denial. However, claims also deserve examination based on the information to which we gain access, and a great deal of public evidence indicates that standard police systems are ill-prepared to competently process claims against the wealthy, the powerful, or institutions that would implicate them. After hacktivist Anonymous declared war on those accused in the "red rooms," many sources reported that neither Anonymous nor its supporters were unharmed. If Jessie's testimony is true, many children and adults are currently being abused. Helpers are endangered. We cannot assume that Jessie is the only victim who has used that specific means to fax for help. We cannot afford to compile our false positives. Instead, we need pathways for prompt, competent investigation.

I still do not know whether Jessie's testimony is true. I suspect, but can't prove, that some version of it is. And if her account is valid, her claims have enormous implications for both Cherem and for harm on a larger scale. Sexual abuse within cults almost invariably occurs across generations. Further, the influential people and institutions that are implicated are incentivized to deny and discredit such claims aggressively. Social systems of this nature function with sophisticated means of perpetuating the community in an altered state of reality in which the abuse doesn't occur. I'm not comfortable yielding to their desires.

Prosecution and defense, as we can see, are the extremes that the judicial system could go to when tried like this, and it would appear that both sides went to great lengths to make sure that it was known that they had no medical knowledge in dispelling myths before this point. Their medical experts were used to address other issues. Today, some professionals are considered experts in medical and behavioral areas and use the basic principles of psychology that are well known to most humans to tell everyone, after completing their education and interning, about unproven aspects within a court complaint, irrespective of proven integrity. With this comes the power to intervene and protect the public from quack methods that have become very prominent and could have severe implications. The professionals who know what these stopping points are and what happens once the fundamental principles have been answered are called psychologists trained on the limits of admitting non-controversial scientific principles during comment testimony.

Detainees or prisoners – This is undoubtedly profound and can get you thinking about its place within worldwide judicial and government systems. Judicial and governmental systems that claim to have the foundation of genuine mens rea in a justice system whose purpose is to provide positive and appropriate discipline using proven and tested, humanistic, and scientifically and professionally accredited principles should control those who are there because of their lack of regard for the benefits of this foundation. This is an essential decisive force in allowing a judicial or a governmental system whose collective checks and balances do not go haywire to transform into something that cannot effectively function. It would be beneficial for everyone if a desired successful change were to be seen in the global justice system if there were some very unique general principles upon which these present justice systems are built, including the mind, the overall totality, that an accused is made up of.

Law – It is disturbing to hear that the points mentioned here are the basic things you need to take to heart when the laws in place are supposed to set down the principles and conditions you should easily be able to comprehend time and time again so that the ones set over you cannot simply pick and choose when to carry them out and have doubt thrown in so that they can operate entirely outside of the model.

In addition, particular confirmations are credible and targeted from several others who availed themselves of and for good purposes – Christian personalities, leaders, and influencers unparalleled, and different kinds of religious men not with goals trying to help Jessie's harrowing testimonies and who are credited with having effectively produced changes in their shame during their testimonies in virtue of the gospel of Christ. Such good faith is justifiable, despite any detractions against the character of anyone who agrees to be part of both groups, since everyone should give them confidence in every respect in virtue of all their testimony about YHWH.

Insofar as testimony, which God inspires, is throughout only in the looks of the Creator and within our hearts and minds, provable, precisely by WORD and eternal truths, in the complete lifespan of the perfect Man crucified and resurrected from death by the immense love of God that delivered us the dangerous temptations of life and death.

In conclusion, it can be logically accepted that the detailed information given in this testimony by Jessie Marie Czebotar refers to several experiences in her childhood and beyond, largely part of her living family, including her mother. Also, a specific scope was passed over by the Minions, subjects of the rhetoric of the New World Order frequently discussed with many others using courses and lectures in the presentations already indicated in this warlike matter. There is no room for doubt that such messages are the relationship of experiences, and as well as she and her followers, she was a gifted girl who evolved into the ideal participant of the powerful Minion House. These scenarios resulted in the enlistment of the disciples to the Satanist sect. At the same time, Jessie was adept at spirituality once she loved and knew God, with an incredible operative. Clearly, her life was deeply affected by many actions as a member of a satanic sect faithful to dogma, which could still be affected if the series of situations outside her family circle respecting many different groups of people were not avoided.

Child Sexual Abuse in New Orleans in the 1970s and 1980s Studying Boy Scouting and Beyond

These cases are of particular interest to me for several reasons. First, they occurred in a single geographic area over less than two decades, thus providing an uncommonly homogeneous sample of specific events of child sexuality. Second, the organization with which many of those charged were allegedly involved suggests how such events may occur through the mechanisms of that organization. Third, two well-known societal custody games are present - problems of defining what happened and who should have known what and did what. These analyses accordingly may be helpful for other such crises.

In the late 1980s and early 1990s, many highly publicized criminal cases occurred in New Orleans. Newspapers and magazines reported that numerous adults who had held responsible positions in the community were sexually abusing minors, both within and outside the Boy Scouts organization. Whether or not the charges are accurate, and the present authors do not know if they are, a thorough review of the files on multiple cases requires an enormous effort not generally undertaken by the media. That analysis is the present authors' task. Here are data-based examples of these highly deviant events from which general insights may be obtained.

Since the early 1980s, New Orleans has become infamous for one of the longest-running civil and criminal court cases involving sexual abuse - the case of residency counselor Wayne Pontiff. This case and its aftermath played a vital role in a long-delayed national exposure of the disorder and extent of child sexual abuse. The volume of media coverage of Wayne Pontiff also illuminated many different facets of society that contribute to the causes of child sexual abuse (i.e., low orphan court budgets for fostering facilities, the distrust and sour outlook of the civil and criminal courts, and the in this case apart times of the 1970s). Given that an estimated 80% of all such abuse is committed by an adult known to the abused child, it's worth considering examples such as the 1970s Pontiff scandal to understand the little-discussed widespread dimension of child sexual abuse - the failure of the victim, his peers, and their guardians in protecting society's next generation. In this respect, the 1970s Wayne Pontiff case in New Orleans is of great significance and remains of paramount interest for studying such future scandals.

The mid-to-late 1980s represented the zenith of the abuse cases. The judicial system had minimal support to protect children. The professions upon which courts relied in the child abuse cases, including psychiatry, pediatrics, social work, and others, were only barely beginning to accept and process the minimal training in child abuse at their disposal at the time of these cases. Although some best practices had been developed in child abuse literature before and during the time these cases were going on, none of these had been generally accepted by the profession. Thus, the experiences of alleged victims involved with the judicial system were uniformly poor, with victims receiving inadequate counseling and support from their attorneys, all while facing enormous pressure from all sides of the criminal and civil trials.

The 1970s, 1980s, and early 1990s were an epic period in the history of child sexual abuse. Sex abuse was coming to light, often for the first time in many communities, leading to national scandals involving the Boy Scouts, the Catholic Church, and other similar high-profile organizations. National headlines were full of documentation of abuse, both in long-form investigative journalism as well as the short news blasts typical of regular news stories. Revealing such disclosures is emotional, convincing the world of their credibility and justifying victims' delays in coming forward. The 1970s and 1980s in America and other post-industrial societies would provide the basic framework for today's revelations and investigations.

The second level of awareness was focused on both sexes. The common characteristic of these levels was to involve the prevention of adult-child sexual relationships. The United States has consistently tried to prevent adult sexual interventions over minors since the middle of the 19th century. The passing of the Mann Act prohibiting the transportation of females across state lines for immoral sexual purposes or the passage in 1891 of a law punishing with diverse penalties, actions of sexual deprivation of liberty (indecent liberties) in minors by adults can be considered targeted legislation containing the initial phase of repression against sex crimes on people under the age of 12.

Even if it was better known and recognized from earlier times, child molestation victimology became a significant social and judiciary matter after the 1970s. Awareness of this type of sexual deviancy can be found in psychiatric, psychoanalysis, criminal psychiatry, and sociology fields during the 19th century. However, attentiveness on this subject began to grow in respect of children from the 70s decade. Legislation in the United States and England on sex abuse and the exchange of relevant scientific evidence on psychiatry and judicial practices created a collective consciousness about abuse committed by adults to children. Considering the 19th and 20th centuries, this societal sensitization could be seen in two levels of protective awareness. The first one involved particularly young girls having greater familial control and broader moral and social attitudes, and the creation of special anti-sex abuse infra-systems of judicial protection against offenders.

Like scout abuse law, New Orleans lacks comprehensive research because of severe jurisdictional limitations. The two school-related instances in New Orleans where decades-old abuse cases received wide attention over the past two decades forced newspapers to search building inspection records and advertisements in a phone book. Elsewhere, with no legislative delegation of investigatory powers or media focus, the extent of misconduct could remain a mystery. But in terms of area children abused, New Orleans politics resulted in a city ordinance that required individuals to register as sex offenders if convicted of certain crimes.

During the 1970s and the 1980s, my research uncovered Boy Scout cases that were documented by the media as having occurred in Greater New Orleans. The sex abuse incidents that were reported appeared in seven newspapers published over fifteen years. Although the number of accused men was fewer in the Boy Scouts than in church cases, the accused Scout leaders had a higher average number of boys abused per man. The geographic scope of the abuse or molestation by Scout leaders spanned the metro area. Other "victims" sued the local council, paying awards smaller than those in lawsuits against the Catholic archdioceses and a church in Metairie in the 1980s. That no previous research investigated this group offers new evidence of the lack of comprehensive research into sexual abuse of boys.

The pioneer years of Scouting are filled with notable events. President Theodore Roosevelt agreed to become the honorary President of the national organization. His 1905 establishment of the nation's first Civic Patrol laid the groundwork for the Boy Scout organization. Ten years later, Congress passed the resolution setting aside as a national park one of the 3,000-foot peaks in New York's Indian Pass. Theodore Roosevelt found this project particularly appealing. We know that he accepted an invitation from the Troop and President Taft to dedicate the park on a family expedition that the Taft children recounted in magazine articles still of historical and emotional interest. New York City's urban boys and leaders became pioneers as well. Today, one of our modern fine young men from the Bronx, Carlos Medina, serves as Scouting National Commissioner.

In October 1910, some 17 boys in Washington Heights gathered at the Washington Hose #10 firehouse on the corner of Broadway and 173rd Street to meet William Bennett. This young man, a British citizen and national Scout Commissioner of South Africa who had recently arrived in the United States to organize Scouting for American boys, quickly enlisted the youthful New Yorkers as the first registered Boy Scouts in New York City. Then, throughout the nation, the Boy Scout organization provided the only major out-of-school program for boys.

Scout programs thrived and expanded throughout the country. Within ten months, three Lodges of the Order of the Arrow had sprung up in New York's Committees, bringing new Scout traditions that would survive and grow to play significant roles in the Scout program. Scout groups thrived in the City's notable Troops, Explorer Posts, and Cub Packs, with hundreds of volunteers providing a wide range of Scoutcraft and camping programs.

The defense subpoenaed Bill; however, he was the brother, and his deposition was read into evidence. The State had called an officer who had observed irregularities at the scene, which he determined indicated the victim had tucked in her shirt. He also noted that the child was crying. An investigator was called as a witness, and he testified that he had maintained a video of the robbery, which had never been booked into evidence. Due to the lateness of the hour, the trial was adjourned at this point. The trial resumed at 9:00 a.m. the following day. The City moved to dismiss with prejudice. The trial judge granted the motion.

Broussard v. State. The first of the cases to be tried was the Broussard case. According to the paper, the boy did not want to attend the meeting, but his father made him go. He arrived at the meeting place and found the lights were out. The police stored surveillance footage in the boyfriend's house of the stepmother a few miles later. On the way to the courthouse, as discussed in the introduction, he instituted the suit. The State subpoena a witness, police Officer Ballard, who had received a report of a little girl alone in the Waffle House at 9th and Howard.

Similarly, the City called as a witness who kept the evidence in the case. Defense counsel entered several stipulations concerning qualifications for different jobs in the Waffle House. The State did not call the victim as a witness. It is called as a witness.

The Jesuits of Loyola University served students from the entire New Orleans area. Their administrators quickly learned that a teaching faculty member there was victimizing a student. However, the order and tradition of a distinguished Catholic high school were maintained at the expense of a child.

The State's training school for boys, Swanson Correctional Training School, was home to a predator from the 1950s until the 1970s. The school was entrusted with incarcerating troubled, delinquent boys. It amounted to a feeder institution.

In the 1970s, there were two schools of particular concern concerning child molestation: the training school for boys and a parochial school serving a large population of troubled boys. In the 1980s, a significant house of prostitution specifically serviced only young males between the ages of 15 and 17.

Boy Scout cases comprised less than one-fourth of the total number of cases of boys who were sexually exploited by child predators in New Orleans during the 1970s and 1980s, which was the heart of the molestation epidemic in the United States. There were other cases as well.

Finally, it is through education that children can most effectively be aided in recognizing and coping with dangerous and inappropriate behaviors aimed at them as potential sexual abuse victims. By properly trained school staff and teachers, and through well-developed curricula, children can learn to resist, report, and respond to situations designed to force them into inappropriate and unhealthy sexual relationships.

Additionally, the school, its professional staff, and counseling services are vital components of the supportive system necessary to assist the child. The school's supportive role is valuable and indispensable because of its unique relationship to the child. Since Louisiana law protects individuals who, in good faith, report a claim of child sexual abuse from any civil damages, such persons should feel comfortable, not intimidated by fear of reprisal from suspected abusers, in seeking professional assistance to verify their concerns for the safety and well-being of the child. Administrators and other supervisory personnel aware of the law function may be less apprehensive of having to report suspected abusers who may be their colleagues, subordinates, or church officials.

School professionals are vital to the prevention, identification, and intervention, and they must assume first-line responsibility for the prevention and reporting of child sexual abuse. Often, they are the individuals primarily to develop the relationships of caring and trust that victims may utilize in this situation. They are responsible for identifying both child victims of sexual abuse in the school setting and suspected adult perpetrators. The latter category frequently includes teachers and administrators working in the schools. In particular, the school professional may be the first person to deal with situations of sexualized behaviors, which may also be the first identified symbol that a child is the victim of a sexual assault.

School professionals occupy a unique position in dealing with child sexual abuse. They are responsible for providing children with a primary education and have an ethical obligation to protect the members of their charges. This dilemma raises critical issues of confidentiality, professional competency, and expertise.

Of the 48 cases against those associated with religious institutions, the abuses were distributed over both non-BSA-sponsored groups and the closely related BSA-sponsored group. There is no significant difference between the number of individuals who participated in the BSA and the number of participants associated with other groups, and there is no significant difference between the number of individuals related to the BSA and the different groups associated with religious institutions. Data are consistent with an equal distribution of those related to religious institutions and those who abuse those associated with non-BSA groups. There is no significant difference in denominational involvement with those who abuse while about the groups of religious institutions. Lastly, as with the Aiki School, data show that the proportion was the highest in the 1980s.

In addition to participation in the BSA, we examine whether an individual defendant was a clergy or authority figure in a religious institution. Of the 300 cases, 12 defendants were Episcopal, 8 were Baptist, 8 were Roman Catholic, 6 were Jehovah's Witnesses, 4 were Latter Day Saints, 3 were Pentecostal, 3 were Christian Science, two were Jewish, 2 were Apostolic, 2 were Lutheran, and five defendants were members of a Protestant group. An additional eight individuals were associated with various cults. Similar to the BSA analysis, the number of defendants with access to a religious institution and the number of cases against religious institutions for the 1970s and 1980s is not definitive. The present data indicate the challenges of conducting institutional analyses for local jurisdictions. Of the 300 cases in our data set, 48 involved individuals associated with religious institutions; it should be noted that there was a significant number of Boy Scout sponsors that were affiliated with Christian and Latter Day Saint churches.

Findings and Recommendations The Catch-22 situation in recognizing victims of child abuse is their behavior in the present and the incongruence in their behavior during the abuse and following. Current behaviors exhibit coping strategies put into place to protect themselves or out of deep psychological scarring. In contrast, victim behavior initially exuded a loss of innocence and a growing sense of secret shame, loss, physical and mental pain, self-distrust, and rejection, often driving the victim to dangerous behaviors. Since disclosure would put the child at risk of further abuse, survivors exhibit complex behavior, facilitating their double life of coping. Trailing into adulthood, survivors may have obscured memories that impact and surface from other associated behaviors. Given the trauma-focused pressure on child modifications, it is essential to remove the child from the danger, and camper discoveries may be too late for some.

The impact of child sexual abuse goes far beyond the victims themselves and profoundly affects the parents and guardians of those boys and the entire family. The range of effects on the victim also includes fundamental trust issues and interpersonal problem areas, inability to engage in interpersonal trust relations with anyone, as well as excessive fear of being rejected by friends. The Clintons and Child Trafficking in Haiti

This paper is a discussion of media reports about child trafficking in Haiti and the rumor that Laura Silsby is an alias for Ghislaine Maxwell. Statements made by victim advocate and researcher Timothy Charles Holmseth, who closely follows a case of child trafficking with the same cast of characters, are used to confirm the rumors of Laura Silsby's real name. The findings of the discussions in this paper suggest the news of the Clintons' involvement in child trafficking would have far different outcomes if the real people in the scandal were reported instead of the name aliases provided for them.

Haiti has been a child trafficking destination for many years. In early 2010, alleged child traffickers Laura Silsby and Charisa Coulter were arrested in Haiti. The trafficking map to illustrate the trends in arrests and accusations was posted online around the same time. The map lists arrests and accusations involving employees or volunteers of the American Red Cross, the Clinton Foundation, the Bush-Clinton Katrina Fund, The New Life Children's Refuge, The Lamb of God Orphanage, in addition to other orphanages, churches, along with missions, and organizations based in Haiti. Of all the places in the world affected by child trafficking, why is it that only news involving central figures of the Clinton political dynasty makes the headlines?

On the ground in Haiti, where one can meet excited travelers from around the world, workers directly involved in infrastructure construction, professionals reunited in the euphoria of false hope, faith healers, and Orson Welles-like media tricks that capitalize on so many dreams of freedom and financial independence; the picture is a little less joyful. This is particularly noticeable in the trafficking of women and children into the "humanitarian aid service industry," which generates enormous profits for foundations, NGOs, government organizations, and so-called charitable institutions.

A popular topic among Haitians is the story of their relationship with former U.S. President Bill Clinton, while his wife Hillary was U.S. Secretary of State between 2009 and 2013. Bill Clinton was appointed the United Nations Special Envoy to Haiti in 2009. When Haitians report on the adverse effects of the 2010 earthquake, they mention the Clintons a lot. One article that captures the sentiment of many was written in January of 2015 and asked quite pointedly: "What Became of the Billions of Dollars Bill Clinton Raised for Haiti?" Indeed, there has been no lack of studies on this topic. A May 2015 U.S. Senate Foreign Relations Committee Staff Report documented that 25 out of the 83 large projects undertaken - that is to say of those worth over a million dollars - represented investments of less than ten million dollars. Another fifteen cost less than $50 million. Over nearly ten years, up to 42 projects were completed - one project a year on average. At most, 9,000 jobs were created for the two million Haitians in the capital. Rescue denied. The political will to act quickly in the earthquake's aftermath needed to be more robust.

While there is beneficial information, evidence, and research on the topic, for this review, child trafficking will be interpreted explicitly as it applies to the underground trade of Haitian children as sex slaves or for forced labor, or worse, known as restavek, whereby the child laborers are forced to work for families as domestic help and are in many cases subjected to abuse, such as emotional or physical abuse.

Child trafficking is the illegal trade of children for their sexual exploitation or forced labor. The Protocol to Prevent, Suppress, and Punish Trafficking in Persons, especially Women, and Children (supplementing the U.N. Convention against Transnational Organized Crime) states that child trafficking is "the recruitment, transportation, transfer, harboring or receipt of a child for exploitation. Exploitation shall include, at a minimum, the exploitation of the prostitution of others or other forms of sexual exploitation. In simple layman's terms, child trafficking is a type of "slavery" where subjects are forced or placed into situations where they are made to provide labor, services, or, in most cases, sexual exploitation for the benefit of others. While the level of enforcement of child trafficking laws and the willingness of governments to use the laws to enforce child trafficking laws aggressively is difficult to quantify, markets for the use of children as forced labor have expanded significantly with global population growth, globalization, and so-called "civilized secular morality" that effectively makes it acceptable to have the use of children for sexual exploitation on the global market.

The main "types" of child trafficking identified by donor interest within particular content regions are below. The emphasis on child sex exploitation in Haitian research has fostered the notion that child trafficking is mainly about the selling of children for sexual abuse. Due to the limited scope of most research, other forms of child trafficking, such as domestic child labor, forced marriage, and the conscription of children as mercenaries, although identified as problems, are provided far less attention. Furthermore, while national and international laws defining "trafficking" are expanded to include any person under 18 years of age, most of the Haitian and global community is complacent in treating the situation as the buying and selling of girls between the ages of 13 and 17 for prostitution.

While the criminal charges are problematic for those focused on child trafficking, it is essential to note that violating Haiti's laws on kidnapping and criminal association does not begin to address the issue of what the Clintons were doing with Haitian children. The public knows nothing about the case being brought against the three women, but it seems as if what the Clintons were doing with the children is being ignored. The fact that criminal charges have been brought does little to address the issue of government officials using their office to take actions concerning children that would result in predatory prisoners being charged and incarcerated in Haiti's "child protection" system. Because child trafficking occurs with such regularity, it is possible to identify specific "types" of child trafficking or traffickers based on a donor's personal experiences and their work with trafficking officials (type 1, for example).

On January 29, 2010, in the immediate aftermath of their January 12, 2010 arrival in Port-au-Prince, Haiti, Bill Clinton and his daughter Chelsea visited an orphanage in Port-au-Prince known as the Orphanage of the Church of Bible Understanding, a church whose home page included church members conducting musical performances with orphans. Ms. Jeanne Bernard Pierre acknowledged that she had approached Bill Clinton to request his assistance placing orphans with adoptive families as quickly as possible.

The allegations and the incident behind them were detailed in multiple signed articles, with publication dates of 2011 and 2009. That indicates some news outlets in the United States had the story but decided not to publish it, regardless of its scandalous nature (coming as it did in the immediate aftermath of Bill Clinton's appointment as the United Nations special envoy to Haiti). Since few, if any, of those who have written about the Clintons and child trafficking in Haiti appear to have been aware of it, we shall begin by describing what happened.

Before the elections, the activists of Fanmi Lavalas and many of their political leaders would come to our first lecture each year to discuss the implications of the teachings of the Aristide presidency for the November presidential elections. Part of the preparation meant assigning class members to the Fanmi Lavalas headquarters in the Cité Soleil or Bel Air neighborhoods. Some did not have to be assigned as they volunteered.

For many years, our number one assistant, Dr. Louis Gérald Gilles, was chief of the Cité Soleil neighborhood police force, a long-time Fanmi Lavalas activist, and close friend and medical provider to Father Jean Juste. Among the students assigned, M. Duté had been armed when Aristide left office in 2004, and unlike the majority of the other students on campus at that time, he did not return home to the provinces. Recent months have seen a resurgence of the commando training going on in the hills above our Baptist mission campus in the Caiman section of Cite Magny, as more and more of the response is that other elected President, Jean-Charles Moïse, must be reinstalled whether rest of the nation wants him or not, by a swelling number of his supporters have left their homes."

"Without the Clintons and the Clinton Foundation, the 2010 election and 2011 inauguration of Michel Martelly would not have been possible. The people of Haiti are suffering the consequences," Dedonné kept saying while we were talking. We had first met on a pro-Martelly Facebook page, but he quickly saw through the pretense. He did not like what I was writing. I was not buying the "positive change" branding of the Martelly and Penn leadership, and Martelly's supporters were attacking me. We had some interesting conversations, and then I stopped using Facebook and lost touch with him. When it came time for the people of his neighborhood to speak, I went to see him, and they elected him as their spokesperson. Dedonné represents the Lamè Phare movement that had organized the protests against Michel Martelly in the U.S. Embassy in 2004. The jokes from the time still circulated, and many reprinted or wrote new ones when they became Facebook "friends" with Dedonné.

The concessions handed out by the Martelly administration were also unfair to the Haitian people. The people in the communities affected by these concessions were only consulted after the lands were given away. They have had to bear the environmental and social consequences of damaging activities. Martelly signed the contracts without the approval of the parliament and without the agreement of the larger Haitian public.

Because of America's economic and other support of President Clinton's recovery mission, there was great interest in the United States (including the Haitian Diaspora) investing in Haiti…However, much of what was pledged was not given, routed instead through Beltway Bandits (disaster capitalists, vulture capitalists, profit-seeking businesses, and other opportunists associated with "rebuilding" countries after natural disasters) to American businesses instead of being given directly to Haitian companies.

Ironically, the company that has made the most public relations benefit from this is the least truthful about its operations. One of the first to answer the question "Just who has created all these jobs" on a website was the Codevi company, saying, "We have." Pro-Clinton future time traveler Jonathan Bush received a share of the profits of Shayari, S.A., a factory in Haiti's northern free-trade zone, from 1998 to 2002 before becoming the head of Riggs Investment Management. The investing public should also know how Riggs-related operations in Haiti could have impacted the firm's day-to-day business. Haiti's elite has not yet decided whether to act as a long-term benefactor to all of society or benefit themselves from their control of the little national wealth there is. However, there are some things they need to be doing. For example, in other countries, 'wealthy' families and people such as doctors and dentists will often sponsor care for the poor through a free clinic, at the local hospital emergency room, or similar endeavors.

Finally, it is necessary to consider the effects on the people and society of Haiti. If 'a rising tide lifts all boats' is true, then positive social side effects would result from economic development. These side effects, the overall improvement in Haitian welfare, are what proponents of the Clintons' programs should be seeking, not the remarks by one person: "Sorry to have let a monster into our country on a U.N. mission." The company concerned has received $10 million from the Inter-American Development Bank (IDB) for investment in Haiti's 'hotel and tourism industry.' A water bottling company received a LIME loan for $1.3 million in Haiti; no specifics were given.

5. Conclusion and Recommendations During Clinton's term, underage crime in Haiti was never taken seriously, and in 2016, no one seemed to have all the figures. Thirty-five children in the Clintons' inner foster care? But foster care in the Clintons' home or Airlift America, Gibault's company, or McWorm's blackmail setup? Things could become enjoyable, and they probably will. Hillary Clinton's memoir states that

her family could do no such things. The Clintons' presidential debate denied the existence of these Clinton Foundation members. Would the U.S. government or the FBI's national Innocence Lost Crusade have deceived the electorate during such a high-level political fake performance to ensure the installation of a second pedo (state-capacity) p-2 Mafia-led government? Should a U.N. peace force be conditionally accepted since 1995? Post-2016 UN accreditation could not have been worse. With his new virtual dictatorial mandate, Jovenel Moïse could again engage the United Nations as their private militia. Their field experiments finally achieved the impossible. Task force Oak-tree could stop sleeping because Haiti is not a psychopharmaceutical city-dwelling illegal migrant smuggling backyard—lastly, W.E. B. Du Bois would have been unaware of the term cause scam and its contemporary abuse under neoliberalism. To sum it up, the Green mayor of Bristol will never become Haiti's next Prime Minister. Peace.

Sadly, in 2016, statistics were published by a bureau that had been scammed. From the childhood well-being technical team? The fact that these three cited Clintons could care for many involved children is freezing.

As fate would have it, for the Clintons, "Dorsinville (2009, 46-7, 96-98) can teach about Caillaud's detection algorithms. At the same time, Pierre-Louis (2013, 103-105) would also do."

One wonders why the journalists from the Boston Globe, Reuters, or the BBC, for that matter, have yet to receive a Pulitzer Prize for their investigative work. They would have been all set with emails from the FBI ledger and published statements from the I.P. Commission on their public websites. However, defending the reputation of the US-led neo-colonial intervention in Haiti had to prevail. The 2016 presidential debate organized by the Media Consortium was no exception. Therefore, the duo was allowed to lie, and CNN, the New York Times, the Boston Globe, and Reuters kept their mouths shut, as in the Clinton case. One only has to remember what Michael Finkel could write about the accolades he received from the New York Times before he met with the infamous monsenhor João Scognamiglio Clá Dias, founder of the Apostolic Society of Saint John. "Please stop creating all kinds of diversion," as he could say. Their signature year would announce Trump and Loketch, the Democrats and Republicans.

Recent decisions by high publicity members of the American Administration regarding housing and reconstruction projects in Haiti – some currently embroiled in controversy and legal activity – employing convicted individuals, along with accusations from remaining witnesses pointing to child trafficking, are raising serious calls.

But is this another completely unfounded rumor dominating the blogosphere or another secret conspiracy the U.S. investigative and judicial system leaders can factually state is just another baseless criminal conspiracy? With reports of child endangerment released by the witness clarifying their claim in a mid-term 17-month sentence, the current silence can quickly come to an end if participating parties are under a public investigation.

Any insinuated sexual exploitation of minors in Haiti – particularly children whose circumstances leave them vulnerable to extreme human rights violations – is intolerable, as have many social media denunciations now implored.

Aftermath additionally includes post-traumatic stress disorder symptoms increasing in frequency and intensity, pain-related symptoms, an undue degree of pain, seeming to have a relatively high pain threshold, and showing an increased emotional response to pain. Abuses have been reported as having little or no effect; some say it has improved their lives, more say it has had long-term subtle and lasting impact, while many have had to seek therapy and still have issues today that remind them of these awful acts that have been done to them. They still experience flashbacks and nightmares about their experiences, but they never leave them.

If an individual had been part of a pair of defendants tried at the same time as co-defendants, or if the discovery proceedings had required the transfer of many non-state actor's investigative files to state legal officials to achieve justice after the offense, the case would have set an interesting legal precedent. It might have transformed the balance between historical state action norms and constitutional protections in the 4th and 14th Amendments, transforming the analysis of the Supreme Court's cases in cases such as Illinois v. Gates. These and the other program implications of this fact touch many individuals who have committed other crimes, those who are alleged to have committed other crimes, police officers, prosecutors, and defense attorneys who represent these individuals, and the protection of children in the legal system more generally.

The response to these cases also led to many significant legal reforms that have had applications beyond just the area of controversial interrogations. Civil commitment and sentencing were altered to deal with many classes of criminal offenders, especially those who had committed child molestation, in response to the historic failure in this area. In the case of child sexual abuse, the responsibility for child protection against the parent was separated from the hope of rehabilitation of the parents when they were charged with this offense. The strengthening of laws involving such instruments as search and seizure and the right to privacy in the home were being redefined and tested. The responsibility for investigating innocent human-causing circumstances of a death and the right to make a formal complaint of police brutality, especially against an innocent person, presented some complex policy dilemmas. The fact-finding functions of the courts were subject to probes related to the proceedings against deceased offenders or analogous civil proceedings.

The Horrifying Truth

Tammy Rief's life took an unexpected turn when she gave birth to Jonah Earl Rief, a bright-eyed baby boy who quickly became the center of her world. At three months old, Jonah moved with Tammy from Colorado to Alabama, where she envisioned a peaceful upbringing for her son. Alabama became their sanctuary, a place of hope and dreams. However, the tranquil life she planned was shattered by a legal nightmare that tested the limits of her strength and resilience.

Tammy's world begins to unravel when Brian Sullivan, a man from Colorado, falsely claims to be her husband and Jonah's father. Despite having no legitimate claim, Sullivan initiated a custody battle in California, a state with no jurisdiction over Jonah's case. This fraudulent act set off a chain of events that exposed the dark underbelly of the legal system. Living peacefully in Alabama, Tammy was not informed of the proceedings, a blatant violation of her right to due process. This failure by the judicial system to notify Tammy laid the groundwork for a series of legal injustices with devastating consequences.

Brian Sullivan's custody claim was more than a deceitful act; it was part of a broader conspiracy involving critical figures within the judicial system. Judges Pollack and Eyherabide, overseen by presiding Judge Kenneth So, orchestrated what amounted to a 'legal kidnapping.' They unlawfully changed custody when conducting proceedings without proper jurisdiction and without notifying Tammy. Sullivan's refusal to undergo legitimate paternity tests in Alabama, where he was twice held in contempt of court, further underscored the fraudulent nature of his claims.

State officials' involvement in California and Alabama hinted at a more sinister operation. Investigations by the State Department and other bodies uncovered evidence pointing to Jonah's kidnapping as part of a black market adoption scheme. Corrupt officials manipulated the legal system to traffic Jonah and potentially other children, highlighting a chilling example of systemic exploitation for nefarious purposes.

In 2013, the fraudulent court records of the dissolution case were sealed without a hearing, obstructing justice and concealing corrupt actions from public scrutiny. This deliberate move aimed to shield the truth. It wasn't until federal forensic investigators intervened that Tammy could file a 2000-page proffer of evidence and a criminal complaint in 2014. However, Judge Kenneth So's decision to leave these documents unfiled perpetuated the injustice, showcasing the deep-seated corruption within the system.

Despite overwhelming odds and numerous setbacks, Tammy Rief has remained undeterred in her fight for justice. Over a year ago, she submitted a detailed white paper to federal officials, including the unfiled 2000-page evidence, to expose the systemic corruption that led to Jonah's kidnapping. Her battle is not just for her son but to shed light on broader issues of judicial misconduct and child trafficking.

Tammy's struggle underscores the urgent need for intervention and support. The journey to reunite with Jonah has been arduous and fraught with legal obstacles. Her plight is a call to action for anyone who can assist in bringing Jonah home and holding those responsible accountable. The horrifying truth of Jonah's kidnapping reveals a dark side of the legal system, where corruption and misconduct devastate innocent lives.

The kidnapping of Jonah Earl Rief is a story of unimaginable pain and perseverance, a testament to a mother's unyielding love and determination to protect her child against all odds. Tammy's fight highlights the urgent need for reforms to prevent such abuses. This case is a stark reminder of the importance of due process and the devastating impact of judicial corruption.

Leading by example is one of the best gifts a parent can give their children in these times. Practicing respect, responsibility, honesty, and a positive attitude sets a powerful example. Parents must demonstrate safe and responsible internet use in an age where children are often alleviated with iPads, cell phones, and laptops. Monitoring online activity, encouraging critical thinking, and setting boundaries are crucial in guiding children through the digital age.

Educating children about the dangers of the internet and teaching them to evaluate the credibility of sources helps them develop critical thinking skills. Open communication is vital; parents must establish trust and set clear expectations. The role of parents in teaching responsibility and modeling behavior cannot be overstated. By doing so, children learn to navigate the world with integrity and caution.

Parents face numerous challenges in raising children today, but it is crucial to go beyond what school educators and law enforcement can provide. Parents can build trust and accountability by modeling behavior, setting standards, and fostering open communication. Encouraging healthy habits and making children responsible for their actions can protect them and positively influence their peers.

The fight for justice for Jonah Earl Rief is not just about one child and one mother. It is a battle against a corrupt system that can affect anyone. Tammy's resilience and determination are a beacon of hope for countless others who suffer from judicial misconduct. Her story is a call to action for all of us to support those in need and work towards a fair and just system for everyone.

The Finders Tallahassee Child Abuse Case

In the wake of the arrests, U.S. Customs Service investigators explored connections between the Finders group and a possible link to organized child exploitation and satanic cult rituals that might have involved young children in ritual ceremonies. The Customs case agent described getting little cooperation in putting together a case against the Finders and the feeling by the Metropolitan Police Department in Washington that the Customs Service was tainting the children with satanic cult allegations. Sister Lucy Atkinson asked Mr. Giles to look into the case. U.S. Customs Service Commissioner William von Raab told the Attorney General's office that other discoveries of abuse of children might potentially follow the Finders case, and this case represented severe potential violations of law. No federal child abuse case was ever pursued, charges against most of the group were dropped, and the Finders returned to their daily activities. Three of the six children either have been or are scheduled to be returned to the group.

In February 1987, the Finders investigation became public when two men from the group were arrested in a Tallahassee, Florida, park on child abuse charges. There was media concern and interest because of allegations that the arrested men were dressed improperly, were disheveled, and that the six children accompanying them had mange, a scam disease, and appeared not to have been bathed in days.

The Finders' existence first came under scrutiny when detectives questioned the six children, ranging in age from two to seven. The children were dirty, hungry, and without protection from the cold. They told the detectives they were en route to 'Someone's' house in Mexico. Many of the unfamiliar words used by the children sounded like jargon. Their mothers were described as 'birth mothers' whom they rarely saw. The children displayed a concerning lack of knowledge about their own identities. Officials estimated that many of the children did not possess the verbal communication of a one-to-two-year-old, even though at least one of the children was around seven years of age. It was discovered that Finders members had examined the children to determine their intelligence level.

The Finders Tallahassee child abuse case was uncovered in February 1987 when two well-dressed men with six disheveled children were arrested at a local park. A concerned citizen reported the men and claimed she saw the children being led by men in only a few states. One of the Finders later said that the men were en route to Mexico but had taken a short detour to explore a park in the state where they had taken residence. The two men in question, who possessed passports, were charged only with misdemeanor child abuse and released with a relatively small bail. It was because of two women who came forward with information concerning the group that the Finders case received national attention. They described the activities and travels of the group and followed the case as it moved from the Tallahassee Police Department to the FBI, to the U.S. Customs Bureau, to the Finders' office in Washington, and finally to a secret CIA investigation.

Early in the morning of Tuesday, February 4, 1987, six adults and six children from the Finders, a group that had been the subject of an earlier Customs Service investigation based on reports about children in Lafayette Park in Washington, D.C. and odd dealings near an old brewery in Glover Park, were found in a van at Tallahassee, FL. The adults were jailed, and the children, who showed signs of ill-treatment, were made dependent children of the court and placed with the Department of Health and Rehabilitative Services. It was quickly noticed that the children behaved better indoors than expected for their ages, had terrible teeth, and appeared emotionally detached. When they were asked what their names were, they could not answer.

During the 1987 investigations of the Finders organization, unanswered questions arose regarding largely undocumented circumstances—political abuse of the investigation and contradictions in their statements, incidents during the arrest, detention, and release of one adult member in a hospital, and whether the children were adequately protected. This timeline is primarily concerned with documenting these major incidents relevant to determining when some of the decisions were made and what information may have been utilized in making those decisions.

The Tallahassee police investigated by going to the apartment house and eventually stopping the two men driving a van occupied by six children allegedly related to the two men. One of the men had with him a "converted TEC military training practice hand grenade," blasting caps, a fuse cord, timers, and a multitude of knives. The police arrested both men and, cooperatively, they agreed to tell the police everything. In subsequent police interviews, a consistent picture emerged from the veracity of the early witnesses' lies, overstatements, and denials. The story seemed too fantastic to be accurate, but no one's story changed. The investigators decided to quickly obtain a search warrant for the Washington, D.C. "game room."

In early February 1987, an anonymous tipster called the police department in Tallahassee, the capital of Florida. The caller reported that two "well-dressed men" in a known "apartment house of ill repute for debauchery and abuse of children" were "supposedly flying children to Washington, D.C. to take children to retired politicians," where the children were "used and chased around." The caller explained that the children were highly drugged and that the children had control numbers "on their backs and not names."

No criminal charge was filed because of several factors. The individuals stated through their attorney that they had been traveling through Florida with the children and adults to obtain military surplus food, available through the General Services Administration or the United States Department of Agriculture. The children had been given a tour through the university in Gainesville, Florida. Child Protective Services in Florida received a report and referred it to the Child Protection Team at the Central Panhandle Children's Advocacy Center. The latter never became involved. It also appeared that the local families were providing for the protection and welfare of the children. No reports of missing children were received from any of these children across the United States.

Furthermore, the Florida Child Protection Team had been contacted by the parents of at least one of these children and informed of their welfare. No one had come forward to claim the child had been found in a local park, but it had been established that the child was not from out of state. When contacted, the children appeared to be well cared for, and the parents stated that the children were part of the Finders group.

Investigations conducted on March 7, 1987, also indicated that no children plus nine adults were on any of the flights he had observed them with. While the general description fit the Finders, discrepancies were noticed in the number of children in the group. Neither the Immigration and Naturalization Services nor the U.S. Customs had any record of the children or adults entering the United States.

Washington. Metropolitan Police officers arrived at about 12:30 hours. They began to interview the adult males who were with the children and to check on the welfare of the children. The men and the children were driven back to the warehouse, and officers toured the facility to check the validity of the information provided by the men. The facility was dirty and unkempt. The general physical appearance of the facility could have sat better with the officers who responded. The conditions presented an environment of severe uncleanliness, which, in the opinion of the officers, was not fit for children to live in. Information concerning the men, the children, and their place of residence was provided by the witness/victim's neighbor, who had been observing the Finders' activities for approximately 13 days before they were reported to the police. She believed that the children were in danger and should be treated because of their physical condition. The observant witness/ victim said that they were dirty and smokey-looking and maybe even frostbitten after spending time in the woods at night. The adults told her they lived in the area and were camping while hiking back and forth across the country. She also said that the children were told to stay inside the building during the day, and she was very concerned about the fire hazard.

The first response to the incident came from the alert citizen who lived in the apartment building across the street from the Finders' warehouse. She contacted the Metropolitan Police Department after she observed several children, who were very dirty and appeared to be undernourished, with two well-dressed, sharp-looking men in the neighborhood shopping for food. The men with the children were well-spoken and had good manners, but there was something odd about their responses to the children, which made her think that they weren't used to having children around. The woman had been a foster parent for many years and had cared for children of all ages, races, and income groups. She knew what children looked and sounded like and liked having them around. The children seen with the men were not part of the Daddy Day-Care Center group of children. The tip occurred early in the morning, at approximately 9:00 hours, on January 31, 1987. Responding units were scrambled to the scene to investigate a report of possible child neglect. These contacts were the very first of an intricate period of police, social service, and hospital personnel involvement with the Finders' children.

Despite the many factional skirmishes over control of Finders' children taken into custody, the potential confusion over the discovery of large amounts of computer equipment, personal documents, school and government I.D. cards, and the unfortunate but not untimely deaths of Finders' leader Marion Pettie and his lifelong ally and co-founder William (Tobe) Terrell, media coverage attracted significant national print and electronic media and public and Congressional scrutiny to the case. In an economy allegedly "failing" due to inadequate consumer confidence, Finders' detractors asserted that Americans might lose their self-confidence. Optimists emphasized that American distrust of government was so firmly entrenched that the spate of stories emerging from the Finders case was unlikely to do any actual harm.

Initially, the Finders case received limited media coverage. However, as information concerning their game activities was released, print and electronic screen media ran stories about "mysterious" Finders. Among the activities attributed to the Finders by Washington D.C. police and U.S. Customs Agents were international espionage, weapons training for homeless kids, trafficking in prostitution, and the enforced abuse and confinement of children. There were hints, primarily from spokesmen for the U.S. Customs Service, that Operation "Ring a Child" was based on information that made these allegations believable.

Given the passage of time, additional speculation and theories may continue to generate growing interest in the case. Buildings or residences worldwide with slight reference to The Finders at any location continue to be cited in secondary sources and recent Internet websites. Efforts to conceal the details and members of The Finders also still exist. Law enforcement today has very different methods for conducting child pornography investigations, and there is now less of a need for such cloak-and-dagger techniques. Certain distortions of the facts that arose in the inquiry remain with us today. The bizarre mistake by Washington D.C. Police Department in classifying The Finders event as a "subversive organization/cult" had no basis, in fact, and this incident is mentioned in various writings by conspiracy advocates as proof of a cover-up or misinformation.

Shortly after the arrests, the possibility that The Finders might have been a highly organized and very mobile criminal organization began to be discussed. In subsequent decades, the perception and misinformation regarding The Finders became increasingly distorted. Several publications and numerous websites have perpetuated false information about this case. The facts about The Finders organization are extraordinary in their own right. The infiltration, surveillance, and handling/subterfuge techniques they employed in the early 1980s were astonishing. Promoting misconceptions regarding the true nature of this investigation distracts from the genuine danger The Finders presented to Sex Crimes officers in 1987 and detracts from the considerable consequences that likely would have occurred to the officers if the operation had been compromised.

Our society's safety, security, and quality rely on continued openness yet reactionary vigilance. While there is and must always be a certain leeway for individual lifestyles and customized environmental living, under no circumstances should our guardians permit the vulnerability of our future leaders, the children, to be exposed to outright societal perils and destruction. Regulatory agencies, whether of the private or government type, must balance themselves between isolation in a vacuum of indifference and an active, adaptive role consensually toward society's betterment. From many perspectives, the Finders clearly illustrate where the children stand in relation to the fulcrum of the balance.

As members of a sophisticated and technologically progressive world, we must never be led by a sense of complacency. Apathy and dependence on others to handle some of the most toxic facets of society will compound those problems, overburden the controlled group, and perpetuate the cycle of intolerance and violence rather than render it harmless. Using video cameras in cases like Finders has established a foundation that will hopefully be emulated. The vitality of constructive cooperation between law enforcement and the media has been sustained by the Justice Department and the Tallahassee Police Department, which are working with the numerous local, national, and international reporters involved in publicizing this relatively isolated case.

The Intelligence Community that established the Finders has an operational relationship with it today. Rewriting Executive Order 12333 was necessary after the exposure of this relationship, and the dangers of creating undocumented intelligence proprietors still cannot be easily dismissed. One significant impact of the allegation of child abuse was the naming of a federal grand jury to investigate the Finders. The fact that a federal grand jury was named to investigate the actions of members of the CIA was only discovered after the investigation had been concluded since this had been kept secret. The core question raised by the Finders case remains unanswered. Why did the United States Government refuse to investigate the serious allegations of crimes against children raised by Customs Special Agent Ramon J. Martinez and other citizens in 1987? The recent cooperation of the Customs Service in providing documents and other assistance was motivated by the original disaster and the potential for new ones. The cover-up will outlive all of us.

The legacy of the Finders case is mixed. The Finders was the first intelligence community proprietary directly linked to the pedophile underground to be revealed publicly in the United States. An intelligence community proprietary is a business established or otherwise used by a United States Government department or agency to work undercover in an administrative area. Although the allegations of child abuse that were initially made against the Finders were believed by Customs Special Agent Ramon J. Martinez and his colleagues to be substantiated, there is no evidence that these crimes were ever brought to the attention of the United States Attorney's Office for the District of Columbia, or that a prosecution was begun.

The Clintons and Child Trafficking in Haiti

This paper is a discussion of media reports about child trafficking in Haiti and the rumor that Laura Silsby is an alias for Ghislaine Maxwell. Statements made by victim advocate and researcher Timothy Charles Holmseth, who closely follows a case of child trafficking with the same cast of characters, are used to confirm the rumors of Laura Silsby's real name. The findings of the discussions in this paper suggest the news of the Clintons' involvement in child trafficking would have far different outcomes if the real people in the scandal were reported instead of the name aliases provided for them.

Haiti has been a child trafficking destination for many years. In early 2010, alleged child traffickers Laura Silsby and Charisa Coulter were arrested in Haiti. The trafficking map to illustrate the trends in arrests and accusations was posted online around the same time. The map lists arrests and accusations involving employees or volunteers of the American Red Cross, the Clinton Foundation, the Bush-Clinton Katrina Fund, The New Life Children's Refuge, The Lamb of God Orphanage, in addition to other orphanages, churches, along with missions, and organizations based in Haiti. Of all the places in the world affected by child trafficking, why is it that only news involving central figures of the Clinton political dynasty makes the headlines?

On the ground in Haiti, where one can meet excited travelers from around the world, workers directly involved in infrastructure construction, professionals reunited in the euphoria of false hope, faith healers, and Orson Welles-like media tricks that capitalize on so many dreams of freedom and financial independence; the picture is a little less joyful. This is particularly noticeable in the trafficking of women and children into the "humanitarian aid service industry," which generates enormous profits for foundations, NGOs, government organizations, and so-called charitable institutions.

A popular topic among Haitians is the story of their relationship with former U.S. President Bill Clinton, while his wife Hillary was U.S. Secretary of State between 2009 and 2013. Bill Clinton was appointed the United Nations Special Envoy to Haiti in 2009. When Haitians report on the adverse effects of the 2010 earthquake, they mention the Clintons a lot. One article that captures the sentiment of many was written in January of 2015 and asked quite pointedly: "What Became of the Billions of Dollars Bill Clinton Raised for Haiti?" Indeed, there has been no lack of studies on this topic. A May 2015 U.S. Senate Foreign Relations Committee Staff Report documented that 25 out of the 83 large projects undertaken - that is to say of those worth over a million dollars - represented investments of less than ten million dollars. Another fifteen cost less than $50 million. Over nearly ten years, up to 42 projects were completed - one project a year on average. At most, 9,000 jobs were created for the two million Haitians in the capital. Rescue denied. The political will to act quickly in the earthquake's aftermath needed to be more robust.

While there is beneficial information, evidence, and research on the topic, for this review, child trafficking will be interpreted explicitly as it applies to the underground trade of Haitian children as sex slaves or for forced labor, or worse, known as restavek, whereby the child laborers are forced to work for families as domestic help and are in many cases subjected to abuse, such as emotional or physical abuse.

Child trafficking is the illegal trade of children for their sexual exploitation or forced labor. The Protocol to Prevent, Suppress, and Punish Trafficking in Persons, especially Women, and Children (supplementing the U.N. Convention against Transnational Organized Crime) states that child trafficking is "the recruitment, transportation, transfer, harboring or receipt of a child for exploitation. Exploitation shall include, at a minimum, the exploitation of the prostitution of others or other forms of sexual exploitation. In simple layman's terms, child trafficking is a type of "slavery" where subjects are forced or placed into situations where they are made to provide labor, services, or, in most cases, sexual exploitation for the benefit of others. While the level of enforcement of child trafficking laws and the willingness of governments to use the laws to enforce child trafficking laws aggressively is difficult to quantify, markets for the use of children as forced labor have expanded significantly with global population growth, globalization, and so-called "civilized secular morality" that effectively makes it acceptable to have the use of children for sexual exploitation on the global market.

The main "types" of child trafficking identified by donor interest within particular content regions are below. The emphasis on child sex exploitation in Haitian research has fostered the notion that child trafficking is mainly about the selling of children for sexual abuse. Due to the limited scope of most research, other forms of child trafficking, such as domestic child labor, forced marriage, and the conscription of children as mercenaries, although identified as problems, are provided far less attention. Furthermore, while national and international laws defining "trafficking" are expanded to include any person under 18 years of age, most of the Haitian and global community is complacent in treating the situation as the buying and selling of girls between the ages of 13 and 17 for prostitution.

While the criminal charges are problematic for those focused on child trafficking, it is essential to note that violating Haiti's laws on kidnapping and criminal association does not begin to address the issue of what the Clintons were doing with Haitian children. The public knows nothing about the case being brought against the three women, but it seems as if what the Clintons were doing with the children is being ignored. The fact that criminal charges have been brought does little to address the issue of government officials using their office to take actions concerning children that would result in predatory prisoners being charged and incarcerated in Haiti's "child protection" system. Because child trafficking occurs with such regularity, it is possible to identify specific "types" of child trafficking or traffickers based on a donor's personal experiences and their work with trafficking officials (type 1, for example).

On January 29, 2010, in the immediate aftermath of their January 12, 2010 arrival in Port-au-Prince, Haiti, Bill Clinton and his daughter Chelsea visited an orphanage in Port-au-Prince known as the Orphanage of the Church of Bible Understanding, a church whose home page included church members conducting musical performances with orphans. Ms. Jeanne Bernard Pierre acknowledged that she had approached Bill Clinton to request his assistance placing orphans with adoptive families as quickly as possible.

The allegations and the incident behind them were detailed in multiple signed articles, with publication dates of 2011 and 2009. That indicates some news outlets in the United States had the story but decided not to publish it, regardless of its scandalous nature (coming as it did in the immediate aftermath of Bill Clinton's appointment as the United Nations special envoy to Haiti). Since few, if any, of those who have written about the Clintons and child trafficking in Haiti appear to have been aware of it, we shall begin by describing what happened.

Before the elections, the activists of Fanmi Lavalas and many of their political leaders would come to our first lecture each year to discuss the implications of the teachings of the Aristide presidency for the November presidential elections. Part of the preparation meant assigning class members to the Fanmi Lavalas headquarters in the Cité Soleil or Bel Air neighborhoods. Some did not have to be assigned as they volunteered. For many years, our number one assistant, Dr. Louis Gérald Gilles, was chief of the Cité Soleil neighborhood police force, a long-time Fanmi Lavalas activist, and close friend and medical provider to Father Jean Juste. Among the students assigned, M. Duté had been armed when Aristide left office in 2004, and unlike the majority of the other students on campus at that time, he did not return home to the provinces. Recent months have seen a resurgence of the commando training going on in the hills above our Baptist mission campus in the Caiman section of Cite Magny, as more and more of the response is that other elected President, Jean-Charles Moïse, must be reinstalled whether rest of the nation wants him or not, by a swelling number of his supporters have left their homes."

"Without the Clintons and the Clinton Foundation, the 2010 election and 2011 inauguration of Michel Martelly would not have been possible. The people of Haiti are suffering the consequences," Dedonné kept saying while we were talking. We had first met on a pro-Martelly Facebook page, but he quickly saw through the pretense. He did not like what I was writing. I was not buying the "positive change" branding of the Martelly and Penn leadership, and Martelly's supporters were attacking me. We had some interesting conversations, and then I stopped using Facebook and lost touch with him. When it came time for the people of his neighborhood to speak, I went to see him, and they elected him as their spokesperson. Dedonné represents the Lamè Phare movement that had organized the protests against Michel Martelly in the U.S. Embassy in 2004. The jokes from the time still circulated, and many reprinted or wrote new ones when they became Facebook "friends" with Dedonné.

The concessions handed out by the Martelly administration were also unfair to the Haitian people. The people in the communities affected by these concessions were only consulted after the lands were given away. They have had to bear the environmental and social consequences of damaging activities. Martelly signed the contracts without the approval of the parliament and without the agreement of the larger Haitian public.

Because of America's economic and other support of President Clinton's recovery mission, there was great interest in the United States (including the Haitian Diaspora) investing in Haiti...However, much of what was pledged was not given, routed instead through Beltway Bandits (disaster capitalists, vulture capitalists, profit-seeking businesses, and other opportunists associated with "rebuilding" countries after natural disasters) to American businesses instead of being given directly to Haitian companies.

Ironically, the company that has made the most public relations benefit from this is the least truthful about its operations. One of the first to answer the question "Just who has created all these jobs" on a website was the Codevi company, saying, "We have." Pro-Clinton future time traveler Jonathan Bush received a share of the profits of Shayari, S.A., a factory in Haiti's northern free-trade zone, from 1998 to 2002 before becoming the head of Riggs Investment Management. The investing public should also know how Riggs-related operations in Haiti could have impacted the firm's day-to-day business. Haiti's elite has not yet decided whether to act as a long-term benefactor to all of society or benefit themselves from their control of the little national wealth there is. However, there are some things they need to be doing. For example, in other countries, 'wealthy' families and people such as doctors and dentists will often sponsor care for the poor through a free clinic, at the local hospital emergency room, or similar endeavors.

Finally, it is necessary to consider the effects on the people and society of Haiti. If 'a rising tide lifts all boats' is true, then positive social side effects would result from economic development. These side effects, the overall improvement in Haitian welfare, are what proponents of the Clintons' programs should be seeking, not the remarks by one person: "Sorry to have let a monster into our country on a U.N. mission." The company concerned has received $10 million from the Inter-American Development Bank (IDB) for investment in Haiti's 'hotel and tourism industry.' A water bottling company received a LIME loan for $1.3 million in Haiti; no specifics were given.

Recommendations During Clinton's term, underage crime in Haiti was never taken seriously, and in 2016, no one seemed to have all the figures. Thirty-five children in the Clintons' inner foster care? But foster care in the Clintons' home or Airlift America, Gibault's company, or McWorm's blackmail setup? Things could become enjoyable, and they probably will. Hillary Clinton's memoir states that her family could do no such things. The Clintons' presidential debate denied the existence of these Clinton Foundation members. Would the U.S. government or the FBI's national Innocence Lost Crusade have deceived the electorate during such a high-level political fake performance to ensure the installation of a second pedo (state-capacity) p-2 Mafia-led government? Should a U.N. peace force be conditionally accepted since 1995? Post-2016 UN accreditation could not have been worse. With his new virtual dictatorial mandate, Jovenel Moïse could again engage the United Nations as their private militia. Their field experiments finally achieved the impossible. Task force Oak-tree could stop sleeping because Haiti is not a psychopharmaceutical city-dwelling illegal migrant smuggling backyard—lastly, W.E. B. Du Bois would have been unaware of the term cause scam and its contemporary abuse under neoliberalism. To sum it up, the Green mayor of Bristol will never become Haiti's next Prime Minister. Peace.

Sadly, in 2016, statistics were published by a bureau that had been scammed. From the childhood well-being technical team? The fact that these three cited Clintons could care for many involved children is freezing.

As fate would have it, for the Clintons, "Dorsinville (2009, 46-7, 96-98) can teach about Caillaud's detection algorithms. At the same time, Pierre-Louis (2013, 103-105) would also do."

One wonders why the journalists from the Boston Globe, Reuters, or the BBC, for that matter, have yet to receive a Pulitzer Prize for their investigative work. They would have been all set with emails from the FBI ledger and published statements from the I.P. Commission on their public websites. However, defending the reputation of the US-led neo-colonial intervention in Haiti had to prevail. The 2016 presidential debate organized by the Media Consortium was no exception. Therefore, the duo was allowed to lie, and CNN, the New York Times, the Boston Globe, and Reuters kept their mouths shut, as in the Clinton case. One only has to remember what Michael Finkel could write about the accolades he received from the New York Times before he met with the infamous monsenhor João Scognamiglio Clá Dias, founder of the Apostolic Society of Saint John. "Please stop creating all kinds of diversion," as he could say. Their signature year would announce Trump and Loketch, the Democrats and Republicans.

Recent decisions by high publicity members of the American Administration regarding housing and reconstruction projects in Haiti – some currently embroiled in controversy and legal activity – employing convicted individuals, along with accusations from remaining witnesses pointing to child trafficking, are raising serious calls.

But is this another completely unfounded rumor dominating the blogosphere or another secret conspiracy the U.S. investigative and judicial system leaders can factually state is just another baseless criminal conspiracy? With reports of child endangerment released by the witness clarifying their claim in a mid-term 17-month sentence, the current silence can quickly come to an end if participating parties are under a public investigation.

Any insinuated sexual exploitation of minors in Haiti – particularly children whose circumstances leave them vulnerable to extreme human rights violations – is intolerable, as have many social media denunciations now implored.

The Town of Lost Children

The Town of Lost Children is a chilling and enigmatic location in a forgotten and untamed forest. It is a place where time seems to stand still, and an eerie mist perpetually shrouds the streets and buildings. The town is a maze of narrow, cobblestone alleys lined with decrepit houses and overgrown gardens, giving it an abandoned and haunted appearance. Veleno, which translates to "poison "in Italian, hints at the dark and sinister secrets within its boundaries.

The lost children of Veleno were victims of a tragic and mysterious series of events that occurred in the town many decades ago. The calamity began with the outbreak of a virulent plague that swept through the city with terrifying speed. This plague seemed to target the children specifically, sparing few. As the disease spread, the children of Veleno fell ill one by one, succumbing to fever and delirium.

At the end of the 1990s, the small and secluded town of Veleno was thrust into the national spotlight due to allegations of pedophilia and satanism involving local families. This shocking revelation led to the removal of sixteen children from their homes, creating a ripple effect of fear, mistrust, and sorrow throughout the community. Twenty years later, a new investigation emerges, casting significant doubt on the original case and raising questions about justice, memory, and the power of societal panic.

The town of Veleno has a haunting past, filled with mystery and sorrow. Legend has it that the city was once a thriving community, home to families who lived in harmony. However, a series of tragic events led to its downfall. It is said that the town was cursed after a terrible plague swept through, claiming the lives of many children. The survivors, overcome with grief and fear, eventually abandoned the city, leaving behind the lost souls of the children who perished. In the late 1990s, reports surfaced accusing several families in Veleno of engaging in ritualistic abuse and satanic practices. These accusations stemmed from testimonies given by the children themselves, who described horrific scenes of ceremonies and abuse. The dramatic and disturbing claims led authorities to take swift and decisive action. The children were immediately removed from their homes and placed in protective custody. The parents and other accused individuals faced criminal charges, and the community was engulfed in a media frenzy.

The architecture of Veleno reflects its rich but sad history. The buildings are an eclectic mix of Gothic and Victorian styles, with ornate yet decaying facades. Many structures partially collapse, their wooden beams exposed, and ivy creeping up their walls. Once a bustling hub, the town square is now silent and dominated by a dilapidated fountain that no longer flows. The streets are lined with flickering gas lamps that cast eerie shadows, enhancing the town's otherworldly atmosphere. The atmosphere in Veleno is one of perpetual twilight, with the sun rarely breaking through the dense canopy of trees. A thick fog rolls through the town at dawn and dusk, obscuring visibility and adding to isolation. The air is damp and carries the faint scent of moss and decay. At night, the town becomes even more unnerving, with strange sounds echoing through the empty streets—whispers, footsteps, and the occasional sound of a child's laughter. Veleno is steeped in legends that both intrigue and terrify.

Locals from nearby villages tell stories of travelers who ventured into Veleno, never to return. Some speak of a guardian spirit, a spectral figure dressed in old-fashioned clothing, who roams the town, protecting the spirits of the children. Others claim that Veleno is a portal to another realm where the living and the dead coexist. Desperate to save their children, the townsfolk turned to the town's doctor, an enigmatic figure known as Dr. Luca Morano. Dr. Morano, reputed for his medical knowledge, was deeply affected by the plight of the children and vowed to find a cure. He isolated the infected children in the town's orphanage, turning it into a makeshift hospital. However, despite his best efforts, the disease proved to be beyond his control. Rumors began circulating that the doctor desperately resorted to unorthodox and dark methods. One fateful night, a violent storm swept over Veleno. Amidst the thunder and lightning, strange occurrences were reported around the orphanage. Witnesses claimed to have seen ghostly lights and heard unearthly sounds from within. When the storm passed, the townsfolk discovered that all the children and Dr. Morano had vanished. The orphanage was left in disarray, with signs of a struggle and an eerie sense of abandonment.

The most infamous building in Veleno is the old orphanage, a sprawling, gloomy mansion at the edge of town. It is said to be the epicenter of the town's curse. The orphanage, with its broken windows and creaking doors, is believed to be haunted by the spirits of the children who once lived there. Whispered tales speak of ghostly laughter and footsteps echoing through its halls. A small, weathered chapel stands in the center of Veleno. Despite its size, it exudes a palpable sense of dread. The stained glass windows, depicting sorrowful angels, are cracked and faded. The pews are dust-covered, and the air is thick with decay. The chapel's bell, long silent, is rumored to toll at midnight, heralding the presence of restless spirits. Once a lively place of commerce, the marketplace is now a deserted plaza with empty stalls and crumbling shopfronts. Once filled with fresh produce and handmade goods, the market stalls are now overtaken by nature, with vines and weeds growing unchecked. The eerie silence is occasionally broken by the rustling of leaves and the distant cry of an unseen child.

Some believe Veleno was cursed by an evil spirit angered by the town's past misdeeds. According to this legend, the plague and the children's disappearance were the manifestations of this curse intended to punish the city. Another theory posits that Dr. Morano, in his quest for a cure, conducted forbidden experiments involving dark alchemy or supernatural forces. It's whispered that these experiments went horribly wrong, causing the children to be transported to another realm or trapped between worlds. A more benevolent legend suggests that the children were saved by a guardian spirit, a protective entity who took them away to a safer place. This spirit is said to watch over the town, ensuring the children's spirits are at peace. Some folklore suggests that Veleno, particularly the orphanage, sits on a thin veil between realities. On that stormy night, the veil might have been pierced, causing the children to slip into a parallel dimension where they are still alive but unreachable.

The Town of Lost Children is hauntingly beautiful and terrifying, where the past and present intertwine in a spectral dance. Its abandoned streets and haunted buildings tell a story of loss and sorrow, inviting those who dare to uncover its dark and mysterious secrets.

In the years following the vanishing, Veleno was gradually abandoned. The grief and fear left the townsfolk unable to continue their lives there, and they searched for solace elsewhere. The town fell into disrepair, with nature reclaiming the streets and buildings. Those who remain in nearby villages speak of Veleno hushedly, warning travelers to stay away. Paranormal investigators and curious explorers continue to visit Veleno, drawn by its haunted reputation. Some claim to have encountered the spirits of the lost children, reporting sightings of ghostly figures, laughter, and the faint sounds of children playing. Others have found cryptic writings and symbols in the orphanage, possibly remnants of Dr. Morano's work. Despite numerous investigations, the true fate of the lost children remains an unsolved mystery.

The story of the lost children has become an integral part of Veleno's identity. Their tragic fate serves as a sad reminder of the town's dark past, and their spirits are said to linger, waiting for closure. Whether viewed as victims of a curse, subjects of a failed experiment, or inhabitants of another realm, the lost children of Veleno continue to captivate the imagination and evoke a deep sense of sorrow and mystery. In essence, the lost children of Veleno are the heart of its haunting narrative—a tale of innocence lost and the enduring quest for answers in the face of inexplicable tragedy. At the end of the 1990s, a small community is disrupted by several cases of pedophilia and satanism. Sixteen children are removed from their families. Twenty years later, an investigation sheds doubt on the entire case. Details The initial reaction in Veleno was shock and disbelief. Many residents found it hard to reconcile these accusations with their knowledge of the accused individuals. However, the sensational nature of the allegations and the involvement of children quickly swayed public opinion. Fear and suspicion permeated the town, with neighbors turning against each other and friendships dissolving under the weight of doubt and paranoia.

The legal proceedings that followed were complex and emotionally charged. Prosecutors presented evidence primarily based on the children's testimonies, supported by psychological evaluations suggesting that the children had indeed suffered trauma. The defense, however, argued that the testimonies were inconsistent and possibly influenced by leading questions and suggestive interviewing techniques. Despite these challenges, several accused were convicted and sentenced to prison, while others faced lengthy legal battles to clear their names.

The children who were removed from their families were placed in foster care or institutions, their lives forever altered by the traumatic experience. The families left behind were torn apart, grappling with the stigma and the emotional devastation of the accusations and subsequent separations. Veleno itself became a symbol of fear and mistrust, with its residents haunted by the events that had unfolded. Two decades later, a new investigation into the Veleno case began, spearheaded by journalists and legal experts who were skeptical of the original convictions. This reinvestigation was driven by advances in understanding how children's testimonies can be influenced and the realization that the "Satanic Panic" of the 1980s and 1990s had led to numerous wrongful convictions across the globe. The investigation revealed that the techniques used to interview the children were highly suggestive and possibly coercive. Experts noted that the interviewers may have unintentionally implanted false memories in the children through repeated and leading questioning. Despite the grave nature of the allegations, there was a conspicuous lack of physical evidence to support the claims of ritualistic abuse and satanic practices. The initial trials had largely overlooked this gap, relying heavily on psychological evidence and testimonies. Modern psychological experts reevaluated the children's testimonies and concluded that many of the described events were implausible or inconsistent with known patterns of abuse. These experts suggested that the children might have been influenced by the media, adults, or their own imaginations. The role of the media in shaping public perception and fueling the panic was also scrutinized. Sensationalist reporting had amplified the hysteria, creating an environment where it was difficult for the accused to receive a fair trial.

The findings of the reinvestigation had a profound impact on the community of Veleno. For the families of the accused, it was a bittersweet vindication; while it offered hope for clearing their names, it could not undo the years of suffering and separation. The children, now adults, faced the complex task of reconciling their past experiences with the new revelations. Some felt a sense of betrayal, while others struggled with the ambiguity of their memories. Efforts to rectify the injustices of the Veleno case are ongoing. Legal teams are working to overturn wrongful convictions, and support groups have been established to help the victims of this ordeal rebuild their lives. Additionally, the case has prompted calls for reforms in how child testimonies are handled in legal contexts and highlighted the dangers of moral panics.

Today, Veleno remains abandoned, a ghost town that attracts only the bravest or most foolhardy adventurers. Paranormal investigators and thrill-seekers are drawn to its eerie reputation, hoping to uncover the secrets that lie hidden within its ruins. Despite its abandonment, Veleno casts a long shadow, and its tragic history and ghostly legends keep its memory alive. David and I hope this book and these chapters serve as a poignant reminder of the fragile nature of truth and justice in the face of societal fear and hysteria. It underscores the importance of thorough and unbiased investigations, the need for safeguarding against suggestive interrogation methods, and the enduring impact such cases have on individuals and communities. As the truth about Veleno unfolds, it challenges us to reflect on the complexities of memory, the power of collective fear, and the enduring quest for justice.

Unsolved Cold Cases, Innocence Lost, and Justice Delayed

David and I have dedicated countless hours to researching and documenting the heartbreaking cases of children and young adults who have gone missing or were murdered. These cases, filled with sorrow and unanswered questions, have left an indelible mark on our hearts. Through this chapter, we aim to shed light on these tragedies, hoping that renewed attention will bring justice to the victims and their families. We also hope that sharing these stories can foster a greater sense of vigilance and advocacy in our communities.

Shannon Paulk

On August 16, 2001, Shannon Paulk, an 11-year-old girl from Prattville, Alabama, vanished from her neighborhood in the Candlestick Mobile Home Park. Her disappearance stunned the tight-knit community. For two agonizing months, Shannon's family and friends held out hope for her safe return. Tragically, hunters discovered her remains in northern Autauga County, confirming the worst fears. Investigators believe Shannon was kidnapped, but despite exhaustive efforts, her killer remains at large. The loss of Shannon left a void in her family's life, a daily reminder of a precious life cut short.

Heaven LaShae Ross ('Shae')

Heaven LaShae Ross, affectionately known as 'Shae,' disappeared two decades ago at 11. Shae's last known location was her home in Northport, Alabama, before she was found dead in an abandoned house in Holt. The circumstances of her death remain shrouded in mystery, with her family receiving few details about what happened to their beloved daughter. Shae's mother, Beth Thompson, continues to grapple with the anguish of losing her child and the absence of answers that might bring closure.

Tabitha Danielle Tuders

Tabitha Tuders was last seen in Nashville, Tennessee, on April 29, 2003. She left home early in the morning, intending to board the school bus. However, she never made it to the bus stop and has not been seen since. The disappearance of Tabitha has left her family in a perpetual state of uncertainty and grief. Over the years, numerous leads have emerged, but none have brought Tabitha back or clarified her fate. Her case remains one of Nashville's most enduring mysteries.

Teresa Dean

On August 15, 1999, 11-year-old Teresa Dean left her home in Twiggs County, Georgia, to visit a neighbor's puppies and a friend. She never returned. The passing years have brought no answers, only deepening the heartache for her family. Teresa's disappearance remains a poignant reminder of the fragility of life and the relentless pursuit of justice that her family endures.

Kimberly Nicole Arrington

Sixteen-year-old Kimberly Arrington vanished on October 30, 1998, from Montgomery, Alabama. Despite the passage of over a decade, her father holds hope for her return. Kimberly's case is a stark illustration of the pain experienced by families of missing children and the enduring hope that they might one day come home. Her disappearance continues to baffle investigators, and her family remains vigilant in seeking answers.

Brittney Wood

In 2012, Alabama was rocked by the disappearance of 19-year-old Brittney Wood, a young mother who went missing after meeting up with her uncle. Days after Brittney was last seen, her uncle, Donald Holland, was found dead from an apparent self-inflicted gunshot wound. Brittney's case is interwoven with disturbing allegations and unanswered questions. Her family's quest for the truth has been fraught with frustration and sorrow as they seek to understand what happened to Brittney and why.

Chanty Shiverdecker

Chanty Shiverdecker went missing on December 9, 1994, after being last seen at basketball practice at Radney School in Alexander City, Alabama. Her remains were eventually discovered, but forensic examiners could not determine a specific cause of death, only that it was a homicide. Chanty's unsolved murder continues to haunt her community and loved ones, underscoring the need for continued efforts to solve cold cases.

Sherry Lynn Marler

Sherry Lynn Marler was last seen in downtown Greenville, Alabama, on June 6, 1984. She left the First National Bank to go to a gas station across the street and never returned. Despite the passing decades, Sherry's case remains unsolved. Her disappearance has left her family in a state of perpetual mourning and uncertainty, yearning for answers that have yet to come.

Kemberly Ramer

On August 15, 1997, Kemberly Ramer disappeared from her father's house in Opp, Alabama. Evidence of a struggle was found, yet Kemberly's items were left behind, including her car and wallet. Her case has remained a mystery, with her family desperately seeking closure and justice. The pain of Kemberly's loss is compounded by the lack of resolution, leaving her loved ones in a constant state of grief.

Carla Corley

In July 1980, Carla Corley was allegedly abducted and raped by a group of men near Lake Purdy in Alabama, just one month before she was last seen. Despite a brutal three-hour attack and the men returning to her family's residence the week before she disappeared, Carla's fate remains unknown. Her case highlights the brutality that can be inflicted upon innocent lives and the enduring quest for justice by those left behind.

Rhonda Dale Byers

Rhonda Dale Byers disappeared from Birmingham, Alabama, on January 1, 1981. Her case remains unsolved, adding to the long list of cold cases that continue to elude resolution. The disappearance of Rhonda is a stark reminder of the countless lives affected by such tragedies and the importance of ongoing efforts to solve these cases.

Haleigh Culwell Whitton

Haleigh and her mother, Kimberly Whitton, were last seen on June 21, 2007, in their log cabin on a forty-acre property. Their disappearance remains a perplexing mystery, with few clues to guide investigators. The case of Haleigh and her mother exemplifies the deep sense of loss and confusion experienced by families when loved ones vanish without a trace.

Tashynina (Tasha) Reese

Tashynina Reese, known as Tasha, was just 16 years old when she went missing on September 1, 1989, in Prattville, Alabama. Her case remains unsolved 30 years later, leaving her family in a state of unending sorrow and uncertainty. Tasha's story is a testament to the enduring pain felt by families of missing children and the persistent hope for answers and justice.

Peggy Chappell

On Thanksgiving Day 1993, the body of Peggy Chappell was discovered wrapped in a beach towel, her clothes folded neatly beside her in a garbage bag. Her skull was smashed, her hands bound, and her throat cut. Investigators have determined she was hit on the head with an iron pipe. Peggy's brutal murder remains unsolved, a grim reminder of the violence that can erupt unexpectedly and the ongoing need for justice.

Wendy Bishop

In April 1994, Wendy Bishop was at her home in the Chisholm community when she received a call from a young female on a payphone. Shortly after, Wendy vanished, leaving behind a trail of unanswered questions. Her disappearance is another painful chapter in the story of unsolved cases, highlighting the urgency for continued investigative efforts and community support.

These cases, etched in our hearts, serve as poignant reminders of the fragility of life and the enduring quest for justice. We hope that by bringing attention to these mysteries, we can keep the memories of these children alive and spur renewed efforts to find the truth. Each story underscores the importance of vigilance, community involvement, and the tireless pursuit of justice.

We urge our readers to stay vigilant, advocate for the protection of children, and support efforts to solve these cold cases. Collective action and awareness can only bring closure to the families and ensure safer communities for our children. Despite these stories' pain and sorrow, we hold onto hope and resilience. For survivors of child predation, we offer a message of empowerment: you are not alone, and your voice matters. Together, we can build a world where children are safe and justice prevails. Let us remember these innocent lives and continue to fight for a future where no child suffers the same fate. Our hearts are with the families, and our resolve is unwavering. Together, we can make a difference.

Satanic ritual abuse accusations

The Peter Ellis Case

In September 1991, a conference in Christchurch, New Zealand, included a workshop on Satanic Ritual Abuse (SRA) conducted by a member of the Ritual Action Group. This event sparked a wave of media coverage that contributed to a moral panic about the alleged ritual abuse of children. The media frenzy, fueled by repeated articles and reports about supposed satanic abuse and a mythical pornography-pedophile ring, set the stage for a high-profile legal case involving Peter Ellis, a child-care worker at the Christchurch Civic Crèche. In March 1992, amidst the growing hysteria, Peter Ellis was arrested on charges of sexually abusing children at the Christchurch Civic Crèche. The media's portrayal of a widespread satanic abuse conspiracy created a highly charged atmosphere. Ellis was eventually found guilty in June 1993 on 16 counts of sexual abuse against children and was sentenced to seven years in prison.

Alongside Ellis, four female co-workers were also arrested, facing 15 charges of abuse. However, these charges were later dropped, and the women were released. The decision to drop the charges against the female co-workers while proceeding with Ellis' prosecution added another layer of controversy to the case.

Peter Ellis consistently denied all accusations of abuse throughout his trial and imprisonment. Even after his release and until he died in 2019, Ellis maintained his innocence. His unwavering denial and the circumstances surrounding his conviction have kept the case contentious in New Zealand.

The role of the media in shaping public perception and influencing the legal process cannot be overstated. The media's repeated focus on satanic abuse and the search for an elusive pornography-pedophile ring involving high-profile individuals created a climate of fear and suspicion. This media-driven moral panic arguably contributed to the zeal with which the accusations against Ellis were pursued and prosecuted.

The investigative methods used in the Ellis case have been heavily criticized. Allegations of improper interviewing techniques, leading questions, and suggestive methods employed during the questioning of children have raised concerns about the reliability of the testimonies used to convict Ellis. The involvement of controversial figures like psychiatrist Karen Zelas, who also played a significant role in another high-profile child abuse case in Wellington, added to the skepticism regarding the prosecution's approach.

In 1994, Wellington Hospital worker Geoffrey David Scott was convicted on eight of 20 charges of child sexual abuse and sentenced to seven years in prison. The allegations against Scott made between 1991 and 1992, did not include the bizarre elements present in the Ellis case. However, the prosecution's reliance on the testimony of Karen Zelas, the same psychiatrist who testified in the Ellis trial, has drawn parallels between the two cases. Zelas' involvement, coupled with the now-unacceptable techniques used to question children, has cast a shadow over the legitimacy of Scott's conviction as well.

The Peter Ellis case remains a point of contention in New Zealand's legal landscape. Many New Zealanders continue to view it as a miscarriage of justice, citing the flawed investigative and prosecutorial methods and the influence of media-driven moral panic. The case is currently under appeal to the Supreme Court, highlighting its enduring significance and the continuing debate over Ellis' guilt or innocence.

The Ellis case has had a profound impact on legal practices and the handling of child abuse allegations in New Zealand. It has prompted a reevaluation of interviewing techniques and the treatment of child witnesses in the legal system. The case underscores the need for rigorous standards in investigating and prosecuting such sensitive and potentially life-altering allegations.

The Peter Ellis case represents a complex and controversial chapter in New Zealand's judicial history. It is a cautionary tale about the dangers of media influence, moral panic, and flawed investigative practices. As the case remains on appeal to the Supreme Court, it continues to evoke strong opinions and reflects broader societal concerns about justice, due process, and the protection of children. The legacy of the Ellis case underscores the importance of ensuring fairness and integrity in the legal system, particularly in cases involving vulnerable individuals and serious accusations.

The Dark Legacy of the Superior Universal Alignment Cult

In the early 1990s, Brazil was shaken by a series of gruesome ritualistic murders linked to the Superior Universal Alignment, an international cult with Argentinian roots. This chapter delves into the horrifying activities of the cult, the prominent individuals involved, and the subsequent legal actions that attempted to bring justice to the victims.

The Superior Universal Alignment, led by Valentina de Andrade, is a cult with roots in Argentina but branches extending into Brazil and even as far as Holland. De Andrade authored a controversial book titled God, the Great Farce, which propagated the cult's beliefs, which included a twisted mix of apocalyptic visions and satanic rituals.

In the early 1990s, Brazilian authorities began investigating a string of child abductions and murders in the Amazonian town of Altamira. The victims, aged between eight and thirteen years, had been subjected to horrific torture and mutilation. Their genitals were removed, allegedly for use in satanic rituals conducted by the cult.

A breakthrough in the investigation came when several prominent citizens were arrested. Searches of their homes uncovered a trove of disturbing evidence: cult registers, firearms, hooded cloaks, satanic publications, and 100 videotapes documenting cult ceremonies. These findings linked the accused to the Superior Universal Alignment and suggested an international network of satanic groups.

Between 1989 and 1993, at least three children were confirmed murdered, and two others were castrated in Altamira. The victims endured unimaginable suffering before their deaths. The organs of castrated victims were harvested by two doctors involved with the cult and sold on the international black market.

The investigation revealed a shocking level of involvement from local elites. Those arrested included a former police officer, a businessman, and the son of an influential landowner. These individuals had paid the cult to perform the ritualistic murders, showcasing a disturbing blend of power, wealth, and depravity.

In 2003, five members of the Superior Universal Alignment cult were convicted for their roles in the ritualistic murders and castrations. Valentina de Andrade, then 75 years old, was identified as the ringleader. Despite her advanced age, she had been a fugitive sought by police in Argentina and Uruguay for similar crimes before her arrest in Brazil.

The convictions marked a significant, albeit incomplete, step towards justice. While the court sentenced the five cult members, including de Andrade, many believed that the true extent of the cult's atrocities was not fully uncovered. Families of the victims insisted that at least nineteen other children had been murdered, far exceeding the number of confirmed cases.

The Superior Universal Alignment's activities in Brazil highlighted the global reach of certain cults. Brazilian authorities suggested connections between the cult and international satanic groups, raising concerns about similar activities elsewhere. The involvement of high-profile individuals underscored the potential for corruption and complicity in such crimes.

The Altamira case remains a dark chapter in Brazil's history, a stark reminder of the potential for evil lurking within seemingly ordinary communities. The cult's actions and the subsequent trials have had lasting impacts on the victims' families and the broader society, underscoring the importance of vigilance and justice in combating such atrocities.

The case of the Superior Universal Alignment cult in Brazil is a chilling example of how deeply rooted and widespread evil can be. It illustrates the devastating impact of ritualistic violence on innocent lives and the complex challenges of bringing perpetrators to justice. As we reflect on these events, it is crucial to remember the victims and remain vigilant against such horrors in our society. This chapter aims to keep the memory of these tragic events alive, advocating for continuous efforts to protect children and seek justice for those suffering.

The Cynthia Owen case is a quest for justice in Ireland.

The tragic story of Cynthia Owen (formerly Sindy Murphy) and the unresolved murder of her infant daughter over three decades ago has captivated and horrified Ireland. This chapter explores the complex and disturbing events surrounding the case, the challenges faced in seeking justice, and the ongoing quest for answers.

In 2007, a jury at Dublin County Coroner's Court unanimously ruled that an infant found stabbed to death over three decades prior was indeed the daughter of Cynthia Owen. The infant's murder was alleged to have been committed by the child's grandmother. Despite Cynthia Owen's request, the Minister of Justice refused to allow the exhumation of the child's body, a decision she did not contest.

Due to the Coroners Act of 1962, the inquest could not assign blame and thus returned an open verdict. The jury was instructed to use a "balance of probabilities" standard rather than the "beyond a reasonable doubt" standard of criminal trials. This lesser standard of proof led to a ruling that did not conclusively determine guilt but affirmed Cynthia Owen's claims about her daughter's identity and murder.

During the trial, Cynthia Owen recounted her harrowing experiences of incest, organized abuse, and satanic ritual abuse perpetrated by her parents and at least nine other men. Her psychologist supported her claims. Owen alleged that her brother Michael and sister Theresa were also victims of abuse, a charge denied by her surviving older brother and father. Notably, Cynthia identified her older brother, Peter Murphy Junior, and her father, Peter Murphy Senior, as her abusers.

The case is further complicated by the tragic fates of Cynthia's siblings. Her brother Martin committed suicide in 1995 after revealing that he had been sodomized in their family home. Another brother, Michael, disappeared in 2002, and shortly after his body was discovered in 2005, their sister Theresa also committed suicide. Theresa's 37-page suicide note corroborated Cynthia's accounts of abuse. A friend of Theresa's testified that she had confided in him about her childhood sexual abuse.

Owen also claimed that a stillborn second child was buried in the family garden. However, police investigations found no human remains. Cynthia has raised significant concerns about the disposal of her daughter's body and the police's handling of the case. Critical evidence, including blood and tissue samples, the bag, and sanitary towels found with the infant, as well as records from the first inquest, have all gone missing. Additionally, Cynthia's daughter was buried in a mass grave alongside other infants, further complicating efforts to seek justice.

Cynthia Owen's parents and older siblings have consistently denied her allegations of abuse. After the Coroner's Court ruling, her father, Peter Murphy Senior, and three sisters were granted the right to appeal. They claimed the coroner was biased in favor of Owen, protected her during her testimony, and selectively presented evidence to the jury. Despite these challenges, Cynthia continued her fight for justice.

The case has remained under investigation by the Garda Síochána. Public support for further investigation has been significant, as evidenced by a petition with over 10,000 signatures submitted to government authorities in 2014. The continued public interest underscores the broader societal implications and the desire for accountability and justice.

The Cynthia Owen case is a poignant example of the enduring struggle for justice in the face of deeply rooted family and societal trauma. The conflicting narratives, lost evidence, and tragic outcomes for several family members paint a complex picture of abuse and denial. As the case remains under investigation, it highlights the critical need for rigorous legal processes, compassionate support for survivors, and an unwavering commitment to uncovering the truth. This chapter serves as a reminder of the resilience of those seeking justice and the importance of systemic reforms to prevent such tragedies.

Creating A Safe Environment Proactive Measures to Protect Our Children

In a world where the safety of our children can never be taken for granted, it is imperative to create environments where they can grow, learn, and thrive without fear. The responsibility to protect our children from predators lies with all of us—parents, caregivers, educators, and communities. By setting clear boundaries, monitoring online activities, and educating our children about personal safety, we can establish a foundation for their well-being.

Prevention begins at home, where establishing a secure environment involves open communication and proactive measures. Setting boundaries and monitoring online activities are crucial to safeguarding children from threats. By teaching children about personal safety and respecting their and others' boundaries, we empower them to navigate their world confidently and responsibly.

Discussing topics such as personal safety and predatory behavior can be challenging, but these conversations are essential. Raising awareness and educating children and adults about the risks and signs of predation helps create a vigilant and informed community. It is crucial to foster an environment where children feel safe to voice their concerns and seek help from trusted individuals, organizations, or authorities when needed.

Parents and caregivers have an essential role in safeguarding children. Practical steps include Creating standards for online behavior. Know who your children interact with—regularly discuss what to do if they are uncomfortable or intimidated. Children's safety education must teach them how to spot red flags and report harmful conduct. Schools, communities, and law enforcement agencies are integral in creating safe spaces for children. By implementing comprehensive safety programs, conducting regular training sessions, and maintaining open lines of communication with students and parents, these institutions can significantly protect children. Collaboration and a unified approach are critical in ensuring the effectiveness of these efforts.

Educating children and adults on recognizing the red flags and warning signs of predatory behavior is vital to prevention. Understanding these indicators allows for timely intervention and protection. By staying informed and vigilant, we can empower children to identify and report inappropriate behavior is a powerful prevention strategy. Teaching them about their rights, personal boundaries, and the importance of speaking up fosters a sense of autonomy and security. Encouraging open communication and reinforcing the message that they will be heard and supported strengthens their confidence to act when necessary.

Creating safe settings for children requires comprehensive methods covering online and offline places. Practical suggestions for parents, caregivers, and educators include Setting parental controls on gadgets and supervising online interactions. Fostering safe physical environments in which children may interact and play. Adopting these procedures allows us to construct a protective network around our children. This chapter will delve into the practical steps and strategies to create a safe environment for children. We will explore the roles of various stakeholders in this collective effort and provide actionable tips to ensure the safety and well-being of our children. Together, we can build a future where every child is protected from harm and free to reach their full potential.

Parents, it's crucial to acknowledge the benefits and risks associated with technology in our children's lives. While computers, the internet, and cell phones offer valuable educational and social opportunities, they also expose children to potential dangers, including online predators and inappropriate content. Let's explore some statistics and strategies for protecting our children in the digital age.

Many parents struggle with maintaining open communication with their children about online activities, which can hinder their ability to recognize and address potential risks. While statistics can be daunting and subject to change, they provide valuable insights into the prevalence of issues like human trafficking and sextortion. For instance, research indicates that 67% of online predators are female, and a staggering 91% of teens have encountered sexual content online. However, only 7% of parents know these encounters, highlighting the urgent need for increased awareness and communication.

One alarming trend is the growing number of young children accessing the internet very early, with usage among 3 to 4-year-olds doubling in just five years. The COVID-19 pandemic further exacerbated these concerns, leading to a 58% increase in strangers attempting to contact children online. Many children are exposed to manipulation and explicit content, with 40% of victims in grades four to eight experiencing online interactions with strangers.

To address these challenges, parents must proactively safeguard their children online. This includes starting conversations about online safety from a young age, teaching children about the risks of interacting with strangers and establishing clear guidelines for internet use. It's essential to monitor children's online activities, utilize parental controls, and educate them about sextortion and other forms of exploitation.

Parents should also familiarize themselves with resources and support networks available for reporting and addressing online threats. Organizations like the National Center for Missing & Exploited Children and the Internet Crimes Against Children Task Force offer valuable guidance and assistance in protecting children from online dangers.

Furthermore, parents must recognize that online predators can come from any walk of life, including family members. Shockingly, 53% of offenders are family members, and 80% of sex crimes originate from social media platforms. This underscores the importance of vigilant monitoring and maintaining open lines of communication with children.

Safeguarding our children in the digital age requires a multifaceted approach, prioritizing communication, education, and proactive intervention. Parents can play a crucial role in protecting their children from online threats by staying informed, engaging in open dialogue, and leveraging available resources. Let's work together to create a safer online environment for our children.

Fighting Child Predators
in the Darkness

Child predators pose a grave threat to the safety and well-being of children. If you suspect that a child is being targeted or abused by a predator, it is imperative to report your concerns to the appropriate authorities immediately. Child abuse and exploitation are severe crimes that demand prompt and decisive action. This chapter will explore the critical steps to take when suspecting abuse, the legal process involved, the importance of prompt intervention, and the support needed for victims.

Pay attention to changes in behavior, physical signs of abuse, or any suspicious activities. Keep detailed notes of your observations, including dates, times, and incidents. Preserve any physical evidence, such as clothing or photographs of injuries. Approach the child gently and express your concern without leading questions. Encourage the child to speak freely and reassure them that they are not at fault. Listen carefully and document their statements accurately.

Contact local law enforcement or child protective services immediately. Please provide them with all documented information and evidence. Utilize national child abuse hotlines for additional guidance and support. Ensure that your report is taken seriously and that an investigation is initiated. Stay in contact with authorities for updates on the case. Continue to offer emotional and psychological support to the child.

Once a report is made, the legal process begins to investigate and address the suspected abuse. Authorities assess the report's validity through interviews and evidence collection. Medical examinations may be conducted to gather physical evidence. If immediate danger is identified, authorities may remove the child from the home or issue restraining orders against the suspected abuser. Temporary placement with foster care or relatives may be arranged. A comprehensive investigation includes forensic interviews, medical reports, and expert testimonies. Law enforcement and child protective services work collaboratively to build a case. If evidence supports the allegations, charges are filed, and the case proceeds to court. Measures such as closed-circuit testimony or child advocacy support are taken to ensure the child's safety and comfort during testimony.

Continuous support for the child includes counseling, therapy, and assistance with reintegration into a safe environment. Authorities monitor the child's well-being and provide necessary resources for recovery. Victims of child predation require extensive support to heal from their traumatic experiences. Access to counseling, therapy, and support groups is essential in recovery.

Professional counseling helps victims process their trauma and develop coping strategies. Therapy sessions can be tailored to address specific issues such as PTSD, anxiety, and depression. Connecting with others who have experienced similar trauma can provide comfort and understanding. Support groups offer a safe space for victims to share their experiences and receive emotional support.

Child predation can result in long-term psychological effects, including PTSD, depression, and anxiety. Early and consistent therapeutic interventions can mitigate these impacts and support recovery. Educating victims about their rights and providing tools for self-empowerment are crucial for rebuilding their lives. Empowering victims helps them regain control and confidence.

Holding perpetrators accountable is essential to prevent further harm to children and ensure justice for victims. Legal actions against child abusers and exploiters are crucial in this endeavor. Perpetrators are arrested and prosecuted based on collected evidence and witness testimonies. Legal proceedings aim to secure convictions and appropriate sentencing. Advocacy groups work tirelessly to support victims and push for legal reforms. Ensuring that laws are enforced and updated to protect children is a continuous effort.

Case studies and real-world examples Operations at Walt Disney Cooperating with the Polk County Sheriff's DepartmentIn one of the most high-profile operations against child predators, the Polk County Sheriff's Department conducted a significant sting operation targeting individuals attempting to exploit children. This operation, conducted in partnership with Walt Disney World, underscores the pervasive nature of child predation and the relentless efforts to combat it.

With over 500,000 online predators at any given time, vigilance and proactive measures are paramount. The Polk County Sheriff's Department, known for its rigorous approach to combating child exploitation, launched a comprehensive sting operation aimed at identifying and apprehending predators attempting to abuse children in the vicinity of Walt Disney World.

Undercover agents posed as minors online, engaging with potential predators to gather evidence. The operation involved meticulous planning and coordination with Disney security and other law enforcement agencies.

The sting led to the arrest of numerous individuals attempting to exploit children. Each suspect was charged with various offenses, including attempted exploitation and solicitation of minors. The operation highlighted the importance of collaboration between private enterprises and law enforcement. It served as a powerful deterrent to other potential predators and reassured the public of the ongoing efforts to protect children.

This successful operation demonstrated the effectiveness of combined efforts in combating child predation. By leveraging resources and expertise, law enforcement and private entities can create safer environments for children. The case serves as a model for future operations and emphasizes the need for continued vigilance and collaboration.

The fight against child predation requires a multifaceted approach involving reporting, legal action, victim support, and proactive operations.

By understanding the processes and taking decisive action, we can protect our children and bring perpetrators to justice. This chapter has explored the critical steps necessary to combat child predators and emphasized the importance of community involvement and support. Together, we can create a safer world for our children, free from the threat of exploitation and abuse.

The Phenomenon of Satanic Ritual Abuse in Louisiana

The aftermath of SRA in news accounts is often over as soon as the alleged perpetrator's case reaches the court system; the media merely loses interest in the case after the hammering and, in the absence of the press giving any feedback from the trial, the tactic neighbors believing nothing was happening is conscience carried out. Afterward, several persons placed under SRA charges will never discuss their ordeals. Several reasons account for this unfortunate self-induced paranoia. For one, a friend who is unknown is fearful of the change of public opinion upon learning about their victimhood. Most generally, they turn down a reporter's interview when it comes time for the trial. Whether the charges of sexual abuse are thrown out due to the lack of evidence or guilt or innocence is determined through a time-consuming court process, everyone in town believes the alleged perpetrator is guilty in the minds of many townspeople. Even though there is no solid evidence linking a previous or current accused to the alleged event, several wrongly accused will forever bear the stigma of being guilty, regardless of their actual involvement in the case due to popularly held beliefs. In all too many cases, former daycare personnel have whispered to news media several years afterward that they did not believe in the allegations of SRA, choosing to undermine the direction of the investigators and prosecutors. Citing as a reason concerns retaliative violence and destruction, silence of the medical and teaching field is also used. While families choose not to question the event with the children formerly placed in the care of the accused sex abuser, townspeople freely gossip behind the backs of both the clients and the caregivers.

This article examines the sociocultural phenomenon of Satanic Ritual Abuse (SRA) reported in communities throughout Louisiana. It outlines the method used to deter the presence of an extraordinary event, then examines how media accounts of allegations of SRA in Louisiana during the late 1980s and early 1990s reflect the presence of significant characteristics traditionally associated with SRA events. In 1983, Dr. Ellen T. Lacter coined the term ritual abuse. Throughout the early 1980s, medical and psychological diagnoses of ritual abuse became increasingly common, becoming so by the mid-1980s. Throughout the late 1980s and early 1990s, allegations of hospitalized children placed in protective care due to daycare-based SRA became sensational weekly events all over North America, as well as in New Zealand and the United Kingdom.

The authors use the Louisiana case as a means of exploring some of the common themes found in stories of satanic ritual abuse. The purpose is not only to describe the case and offer an explanatory analysis but also to understand how this level of irrationality and paranoia can be approached and its prevalence can be reduced. This paper is not about whether true believers or skeptics are out there. It is about the phenomena. The line running through the paper does not pit those who know satanic cults exist on one side and those whose brains have fallen out on the other, with sociologists, psychologists, or history foremost or anthropologists somewhere between. Instead, the line is: What can we understand about people who say they have suffered from satanic cults, and what kinds of circumstances seem to foster this belief and unlock the phenomenological difference between the label and the feared act?

This paper first describes the details of the DeSoto Parish satanic ritual abuse case. Second, the paper will detail the societal and religious context in which DeSoto Parish exists and will suggest that historical, political, and religious forces in Louisiana uniquely foster this type of sexual abuse. Third, informed by the commentary on false allegations of SRA, the paper will suggest that it is crucial to examine this form of child abuse within a broader social, rather than strictly criminal/clinical, context.

In the fall of 1997, a small Louisiana parish named DeSoto made national news when evidence surfaced that deputies of the local sheriff's office had engaged in ritualistic sexual abuse of children related to the satanic cult that they were a part of. Interestingly, the discovery of this case coincided with the end of a period of fevered alarm over so-called "satanic ritual abuse" cases, a type of child abuse perpetrated by ritualistic cults usually felt to be disguised neo-pagan or satanic groups.

These ritualistic activities are always carried out in secret settings, with participants actively participating in the preparations and ceremonies. Perpetrators of ritualistic abuse are relatively well-organized and disciplined groups, always charismatic and autocratic to their followers. Deep traumatization at all levels of the victims dominates the ceremonial activities. People take the risk because they feel involved or are committed through blackmail. The practical purpose of ritualistic criminal behavior is not mass hypnosis, the recruitment of drug addicts, the bondage of scared ghost hunters, the commission of atrocities in populated places, or unchecked control of events. Ritualistic activities are focused on the action itself. The act is the objective, and the ritualistic activities are vehicles, pathways, and ceremonial keys shaping the acts. Community effort will break the keys.

Defining satanic ritual abuse encompasses the most challenging aspect of this presentation. Satanic ritual abuse involves cults that may or may not base their beliefs on older religions that are now considered pagan, such as Wicca or Santeria, or on quasi-Satanic church groups that worship Satan in the Christian sense of the word, using blood sacrifices and other rituals that incorporate black magic and other occult practices. Non-organized satanic criminal activities, such as drug dealing networks involved in ritual abuse, are not included as such. Neither is substance abuse, child sex abuse, various teaching and training processes, healing practices, etc., even though these may consist of dark magical rituals. The criminal aspect is the focus here. Furthermore, in the criminal cases underlined, the commercial element, currency exchange, is the core issue.

I will describe in detail the workings of the physical site that formerly existed at Manchac and its historical antecedents. Manchac is illustrative of SRA (or pseudo-SRA) sites that do indeed exist in Louisiana, as well as in other states. This is not to say, however, that sites with celtic connections (dilapidated houses, burned-out churches, and the like) cannot quickly become the focus of popular lore—just as did the current site at Manchac—once rumors of human sacrifice begin to spread or once a vital element of the supernatural is perceived to be connected with it. The ruins of Manchac have been host to numerous tall tales among the local population for nearly 200 years. Moreover, because the Baby Jane Doe case was never officially solved, the story had an inherent mystery that had the potential to capture the attention of the general public, along with the macabre trappings associated with cult activity.

"The Phenomenon of Satanic Ritual Abuse in Louisiana"

This essay discusses the phenomenon of Satanic ritual abuse and the tension between religious freedom and child welfare in the context of this case.

Family and the Bernard children of Veronica Bernard disclosed multiple detailed confessions to members of her family of extreme acts of abuse and a former foster parent of Austin during that confines. The Austin Trey Bernard case also documented a detailed extensive history of DCFS custody, psychiatric illness, educational disability, and early deaths of Veronica and great-grandfather, Veronica, Nate, and great-grandmother.

Recently, two "family kidnappings" of two little toddlers from a different conception and different families have occurred. During a forty-five-day period, Great Grandmother failed to display the requested documents for inquiry into the investigation and failed to display the documents required and ordered during the case history; great-grandfather provided faultless and observed testimony that led to the testimony of not being a fan member of the 26 members of the cult of whom Austin Bernard has been linked to as being involved in a Satanic cult after her adoption on September 5, 1994.

The case has broken over a twenty-six-year period at the hands of the Bernard family. One of Austin's siblings, Melissa Bernard's daughter, the birth mother of her family, has been returned to the Bernard family. Decades of custody and mental health cases have been settled or closed.

During the Louisiana Lafayette Parish Police Department and the Lafayette Parish coroner's office's investigation, the Bernards provided a statement that they were participants in a Satanic cult and they were isolating themselves from Satan to keep Austin safe while he was in the hospital.

On May 10, 1993, Austin Trey Bernard, the oldest child of Veronica and Paul Bernard, was critically injured and rushed to the hospital. Austin was pronounced dead on May 11, 1993. The evidence in the case suggests that Austin had been shaken violently and thrown into a deadly fall.

Briefly, SRA qua 'condition' is not confined to any belief structure or organized religious order conventionally recognized or considered. The suspected and alleged offenders of the East Feliciana Parish believe that there existed purely normative reasons sanctioned by religious and criminal statutes to torture and kill children. Written and verbal disclosures – those formal and informal solicited during the investigation and as demonstrated in the multiple communications with LEOs maintained by the central figure, Leslie – provide notable detail surrounding the motivations for the alleged offenses then and since. These communications communicate the notion of shifting religious loyalties and choosing those others would find morally irreconcilable, thus tempering or precluding condemnation from an otherwise federal, state, or local authority.

SRA was the crux of initial and subsequent investigations into the Dixie Fire. As the status of my inquiry concerns events and persons peripheral to the fire, it also encompasses the phenomenon of SRA, specifically as expressed in the lives of those impacted by and those crucially involved in this investigation. Despite perceptions of credibility and prevalent association with such occurrences about high-profile cases like the Jonestown Massacre or Waco Siege, expressions of SRA frequently find examination and treatment within and at the regional and local levels than they do with more extensive, systemic religious practices. This case challenges the utility of existing conventions surrounding historical and contemporary forms of SRA and leads to the conclusion that such designations are transient symptomology affixed to the descriptions of deviant acts and not necessarily the scope and weight of their impact on victims of criminal violence.

What we can learn from the previous experiments and studies is that evidence of SRA is hard to come by. It is not as common as we might like these days to see some examples of the behavior of some of the people and organizations who are seen as vile Satanic worshippers and their followers in the movies. One thing to be learned from the studies is that SRA may be more about who we wish these people to be than they are. Farid and Zaragoza interviewed college students who were enrolled in psychology and education classes and who had seen media propaganda about SRA. The research found that the subjects believed in the existence of Satanic ritual abuse. These people were not the only ones who seemed to believe in the myth without evidence. During the first half of the eighties, a snowball effect resulted.

Teachers assigned 150 students to watch an SRA lecture to watch another unrelated set of parents and students. Both groups were then asked at random which lecture they watched. The children who watched the SRA lecture performed no better than the control groups. In another experiment, 150 adult students were asked to quickly read a series of articles, some with no SRA content, some with pill labels, and some with SRA essays. As before, the adults were questioned about the content of the articles and could not pick out which had SRA information in them. Another study looked at 12 psych-anthropology classes. A lecture on SRA was given, yet out of 268 students, a total of 121 could not assess the lecture's credibility, nor could they provide any evidence of an agenda behind the myth.

Media reports of recovered repressed memories of SRA have brought questions about the validity of memory. This discussion has, for the most part, remained within the academic community, still working out the parameters of abuse and the validity and liability of therapists, insurers, etc. It is presented here in this report partly because the information is so new and alien from the experience of those who may hear it that it can arouse emotion, rhetoric, and judgment that sets up the accused as convicted with the accusations. And so the sentence of excommunication is rendered without the benefit of trial. Changes have been made legally, and attitudes toward children and their court testimony have changed. Those changes have come through the experience of seeing young children testify in a much more receptive context to their evidence without providing the child the added burden of proving that an event that others had witnessed could stop it from happening. SRA is different. Witnesses still have not been located, and those who report their experiences have no corroborating evidence. And so, the response in many quarters has been, let us err on the side of the children. Adults have no problem believing that intruders can and are sexually penetrating our grandchildren. Why, then, are many of those same people so quick to deny the possibility of ritualistic abuse? We remain quick to accept reports of those who tell stories of children secretly watching the brutal death or dismemberment of many animals. Still, those tales of violence are mirrored by near-total denial of the possibility of ritualistic abuse of those same children.

The impact of the reports of SRA is vast. The effects on the individuals whose memories are "recovered" from hypnosis or other memory retrieval techniques will be discussed below. However, our focus is on the response from various parts of the community. Adults believed to be perpetrators of such activity are the targets of motions in court to bar them from seeing their children. Citizens have made threats to disclose their suspicions to employers and neighbors of people who may be involved in cult activities. Investigating officers are criticized when their final report concludes that there is no foundation to the accusations and that no supporting evidence of ritual activity is found. Therapists who encourage the recovery of memories to develop a client's following are subjects of critique. Media reports that start by quoting experts who declare that they have never seen a convincing case of SRA end with accounts that serve to arouse further fear and concern that an unknown number of those around us are implicated in this evil. Tabloid items inform those in hiding that they have proof that SRA is real and encourage them to escape, revealing themselves to reporters so that their stories can be made public.

Particularly troubling about many of the cases, even when they were dropped or acquitted because of the lack of evidence, is that the stigma of being accused of child abuse stuck and followed people beyond the halls of the legal system. The daycare workers who had been accused were also charged and tried. Only four were convicted, and two of the convictions were later overturned for reasons such as leading and suggestive, repetitive questions to the children and the absence of evidence such as signs of sexual acts. However, many daycare employees also pleaded guilty, in many cases, to reduced charges for reasons such as fear that juries might wrongly convict them when they were innocent. Still, one of their colleagues had incriminating evidence. These workers were ordered to apologize, which some parents found unsatisfying, as well as sentenced to extensive prison terms, some of them as long as twenty or twenty-five years, and they had to register as sex offenders and face significant fines. Then there were the girls who were accused of being the abusers, who were tried along with their family members. The lasting effects of the charges could not be deleted or sealed from their record.

The legal and social repercussions of the accusations of Satanic ritual abuse in the state of Louisiana have been numerous and severe. How these repercussions were managed by the state and how individuals and their families who were caught amid the ordeal were treated raises some troubling questions about the legal and social system through which difficulties were handled—the list of people who suffered legal penalties after the scandal was long. To name just a few individuals, there were the five women who were accused of being involved in Satanic activity at Hosanna Church, who were arrested on allegations of aggravated rape and cruelty against a person with mental disabilities, as well as the nurse who was accused of facilitating these activities, and the nurse who was accused of not reporting them.

In no way do we mean to suggest that there is no such thing as ritual abuse. Indeed, the similarity between the two is stunning when comparing the now-invalidated claims to stonewalled court cases. The removal of SRA elements does not at all diminish the evidence of brutal physical abuse but instead brings it into clear, gut-wrenching focus. In watering down ritual abuse as gang initiation or ritual abuse as MSBP to ritual abuse, and finally, to non-ritual abuse, the vividness of the true horror has been intensified with clarity. Those who suggest that no ritual abuse exists have little knowledge of cases such as the sexual assault of children by court-appointed custodians or ritualistic abuse by daycare providers. Their world is far too constrained.

In general, we see little difference between the elements that were portrayed to be SRA by Christian leaders and the elements of non-satanic ritual abuse presented in recent court cases. Although the legal infrastructure of the SRA scares has melted under the fire of open court procedures, the crimes of non-SRA ritual abuse perpetrators are not fictitious. On the contrary, with the SRA labels peeled away, the actual victimization is all the more apparent. Those who sought to help under the banner of SRA prevention must transfer the dedication, compassion, and broad perspectives that the SRA generated scares to the wider issues of domestic violence, child abuse, and abuse by professionals - and caution themselves that if abuse is not attributed to a Satanic conspiracy, it is nevertheless a severe deadly crime.

The study did not find a network of Satanic cults within Louisiana, as defined. It did find groups of high priests/priestesses who claimed Witch or religious titles that they were or that other people gave them. It is not a violation of the First Amendment for law enforcement agencies to process evidence for illegal acts. Indeed, as long as probable cause exists and proper procedures are instituted, they have a legal responsibility to do so in the process of protecting public peace, safety, morals, health, and welfare.

Several people who had never revealed the cult before provided information about it in a trusted, non-threatening environment, including one mother who reported cult activity within her family. She did not report previously for fear of losing her children and out of fear of the cult. Two prohibited transportation acts across state lines by uncles were described by people with information about the cult. Another reported the death cult's intent to kill four United States senators, but it read like a sci-fi script. No murders were known to be committed.

The term "Satanic Ritual Abuse" was not used spontaneously by 532 children and adults from different parts of Louisiana when they provided information concerning what was done to them in cult abuses. Under substance abuse evaluations, into suspected or known child protective agencies, during rape evaluations, within a general population, or detailed assessments of incestuous molestation, we found only three children and three adults who revealed cults that harmed them openly admitted the cults claimed to be Satanic or followers of the devil.

The Mystery of Chickenwackers

The name "Chickenwackers" evokes a sense of dread and curiosity in the shadowy corners of urban legends and whispered conspiracies. To some, Chickenwackers represents a sinister amalgamation of Illuminati-like secrecy and Satanic malevolence. To others, it is merely a bogeyman conjured by the fevered imaginations of meth users. This chapter delves into the murky past and complex web of rumors surrounding Chickenwackers, from alleged human sacrifices to psychological mind games against their supposed enemies.

The origins of Chickenwackers are shrouded in mystery, with no definitive account of its inception. Some claim it began as a secret society in the early 20th century, drawing inspiration from occult practices and esoteric knowledge. According to specific sources, the group initially formed as an offshoot of a larger, more established secret society, breaking away to pursue darker and more forbidden paths.

The name "Chickenwackers" itself is enigmatic, possibly a code or an inside joke among its members. Some believe it to be a corruption of an ancient term or a moniker meant to distract and confuse. Others suggest that the name might be derived from an old folklore tale, where "chicken" symbolizes innocence and "walkers" connotes those who destroy it, hinting at the group's sinister intentions.

Symbolism plays a crucial role in Chickenwackers lore. Allegedly, the group adopts a variety of cryptic symbols, merging Illuminati iconography—such as the all-seeing eye and the pyramid—with darker, Satanic imagery like inverted pentagrams and goats' heads. These symbols are said to adorn secret meeting places, personal artifacts of members, and even clandestine tattoos. It is whispered that members communicate through these symbols, leaving them in graffiti, carved into trees, or hidden in plain sight within urban landscapes. Such pervasive use of symbolism creates a sense of unity among members and instills fear and curiosity among outsiders.

One of the most persistent and horrifying rumors about Chickenwackers is their supposed involvement in human sacrifices. Accounts vary wildly, but the core of the story remains the same: deep in secluded forests or hidden urban catacombs, the group conducts rituals that culminate in the sacrifice of an innocent victim. Witnesses describe these ceremonies as elaborate and gruesome, with chanting, bloodletting, and the invocation of dark forces.

The rituals are said to follow a strict protocol, beginning with the selection of a victim, often described as someone marginalized by society and unlikely to be missed. The chosen individual is then subjected to a series of psychological and physical tortures designed to break their will and spirit. These preparatory stages are meant to prepare the victim for the final sacrifice, heightening the terror and intensity of the ritual. Participants allegedly wear hooded robes and masks, their identities concealed as they chant in an unknown language, invoking entities beyond human comprehension.

Despite numerous investigations and searches, concrete evidence of such rituals has yet to be uncovered. Skeptics argue that these stories are fabrications designed to instill fear and control through myth. However, the lack of evidence has done little to quell the rumors; if anything, it has enhanced the group's terrifying mystique. The chilling tales of dark rituals serve as a potent warning, reinforcing the group's feared reputation and ensuring their legend lives on.

Beyond physical rituals, Chickenwackers is reputed to engage in psychological mind games against its perceived enemies. Former members and alleged victims tell tales of harassment that verge on the supernatural. They describe experiences of gaslighting, sleep deprivation, and eerie coincidences that suggest a pervasive and evil influence.

Targets of these psychological attacks report a consistent pattern: they might receive anonymous, cryptic messages or experience inexplicable disturbances at their homes. Lights flicker, strange noises are heard, and personal belongings are moved or disappear altogether. Victims describe feeling watched, a constant, oppressive presence that wears down their mental defenses. In some cases, they claim their personal information was used against them in ways that seemed designed to drive them to madness, such as revealing deeply personal secrets or orchestrating events to make them appear paranoid to others.

These tactics echo methods used by cults and secret societies throughout history, blending fear and confusion to maintain control and silence dissent. Psychological warfare isolates and destabilizes the target, making them more susceptible to manipulation and control. The pervasive fear and paranoia induced by these tactics ensure that even those who escape the group are forever haunted by its shadow.

In more contemporary settings, Chickenwackers has taken on a new role as a bogeyman for meth users. Law enforcement and community workers in areas ravaged by methamphetamine abuse report hearing paranoid delusions involving Chickenwackers. Users, caught in the throes of meth-induced psychosis, often claim to see Chickenwackers members stalking them or orchestrating their downfall.

These accounts are typically dismissed as drug-induced hallucinations. Yet, the consistency and detail in these stories across different regions and demographics suggest a more profound cultural imprint. The imagery of Chickenwackers as sinister figures preying on the vulnerable resonates deeply within these communities, blurring the line between myth and reality. Whether real or imagined, the figure of Chickenwackers looms large in the nightmares of those on the fringes of society.

The true nature of Chickenwackers remains elusive, straddling the line between myth and reality. The group's existence and activities are difficult to substantiate, wrapped in layers of legend and paranoia. What can be discerned is the powerful impact of these stories on the collective psyche.

Chickenwackers serves as a modern cautionary tale, embodying fears of the unknown, the corrupting influence of secret societies, and the depths of human cruelty. It is a mirror reflecting society's anxieties and a testament to the enduring power of folklore in shaping our understanding of good and evil.

Whether Chickenwackers is a genuine occult group, a product of mass hysteria, or a combination of both, its legend continues to thrive. As with all great mysteries, the truth may be more complex and disturbing than the myths surrounding it. In the labyrinthine corridors of conspiracy and rumor, Chickenwackers remain an enigma, challenging our perceptions and stirring our deepest fears.

The Sinister Influence of Satanism in Hollywood

The glitz and glamor of Hollywood often mask a darker reality lurking beneath the surface. While the world marvels at the stars that shine so brightly on the silver screen, there exists a shadowy realm where whispers of sinister rituals and malevolent forces abound. In this chapter, we delve deep into the influence of Satanism in Hollywood, peeling back the layers of deception to reveal the chilling truth behind the facade of fame and fortune.

For decades, the tantalizing allure of Hollywood has captivated the world's imagination, drawing countless dreamers to its glittering shores in pursuit of fame and fortune. Yet, beneath the shimmering facade of red carpets and flashing cameras lies a shadowy underbelly steeped in secrecy and intrigue.

Speculation regarding the presence of Satanism in Hollywood has long lingered like a whisper in the wind, with tales of clandestine gatherings and occult rituals circulating among the industry's insiders and outsiders alike. These rumors, fueled by whispered conversations in dimly lit corners and sensational headlines in tabloid magazines, have cast a veil of mystery over Tinseltown, obscuring the truth from prying eyes.

But amidst the chaos of speculation and hearsay, a bold and courageous few have dared to venture where others fear to tread. Metaphysician David and I, armed with a relentless pursuit of truth, have dedicated ourselves to unraveling the enigma of Satanism's influence in Hollywood. Our research boldly ventures into this shadowy realm, unearthing the ways in which Lucifer and his minions exert their insidious influence over the elite of Tinseltown.

With unwavering determination, we peel back the layers of deception, exposing the intricate web of influence that binds the entertainment industry to the dark forces that lurk within. Through tireless research and meticulous investigation, we shine a light into the darkest corners of Hollywood, illuminating the sinister machinations that operate beneath the surface.

From whispered conversations in exclusive clubs to shadowy meetings held under the cover of night, our research delves deep into the heart of darkness that permeates the entertainment industry. We uncover chilling revelations of secret cults and occult practices, shedding light on the ways in which morality is sacrificed in the pursuit of power and prestige.

As we continue our quest to unveil the influence of Satanism in Hollywood, our work serves as a beacon of truth in a world shrouded in deception. Though the journey is fraught with danger and uncertainty, we remain steadfast in our commitment to exposing the truth, no matter the cost. For only by confronting the darkness can we hope to banish it from our midst and restore light to the heart of Tinseltown.

Within the bustling streets of Hollywood, a darker truth lurks beneath the surface of glamor and fame. Powerful industry insiders and well-known comedians, cloaked in the trappings of success, are rumored to prowl the shadows, seeking out the vulnerable and the lost. These individuals, ensnared by the seductive allure of Luciferian promises, become predators in their own right, preying upon those who dare to dream amidst the harsh reality of the city of angels.

Among the most vulnerable are the transient youth, adrift in a sea of uncertainty and desperation. Cast aside by society, these young souls wander the streets in search of solace and salvation, only to find themselves ensnared in the web of deceit woven by those who promise them a way out. Drawn in by the false promises of fame and fortune, they become easy targets for the manipulative machinations of those who would exploit their innocence for their own gain.

Behind the glimmering facade of Hollywood lies a culture of exploitation and abuse, where the dreams of the innocent are sacrificed on the altar of ambition. The Luciferian practitioners who roam the streets in search of their next victim are not content to merely fulfill their own desires—they revel in the destruction of innocence, savoring the power they wield over those who dare to dream.

But amidst the darkness, a glimmer of hope remains. For every soul that is lost to the predators of Hollywood's elite, there are those who refuse to be silenced, who dare to speak out against the injustices that plague the industry. Through their bravery and resilience, they shine a light into the darkest corners of Tinseltown, exposing the truth that lies beneath the surface and fighting to reclaim the innocence that has been stolen away.

As the predators continue to prowl the streets of Hollywood, seeking out their next victim, the battle for the soul of the entertainment industry rages on. But with each revelation and each act of defiance, the veil of deception is lifted ever so slightly, revealing the darkness that lies beneath. And though the road ahead may be long and fraught with danger, the light of truth will always prevail in the end.

In the hallowed halls of Hollywood's elite, a dark and chilling truth lies hidden from the prying eyes of the world. It is a truth that David and I have uncovered through our relentless pursuit of the sinister forces that lurk within the entertainment industry—the truth of blood sacrifices performed by those in positions of great power.

Cloaked in the veneer of respectability, these individuals, whose names adorn the marquees of fame and fortune, engage in unspeakable acts to satiate their insatiable thirst for wealth and energy. Behind closed doors, away from the prying eyes of the public, they gather in secret to partake in dark rituals that defy the bounds of morality and humanity.

The illusion of innocence that surrounds the entertainment industry is shattered in the face of these chilling revelations, exposing the sinister underbelly that lurks beneath the surface. No longer can the glittering facade of Hollywood's glamor mask the truth of the darkness that lies within, for David and I have seen firsthand the depths to which those in power will sink in their relentless pursuit of dominance and control.

But even as we confront the horrors of these blood sacrifices, we are reminded that our work is far from over. For every revelation brings us closer to uncovering the full extent of the darkness that permeates the entertainment industry, and with each step forward, we draw ever closer to exposing the truth to the world.

Though the price of power may be steep, and the sacrifices made in its pursuit unspeakable, we remain undeterred in our mission to shine a light into the darkest corners of Tinseltown. For only by confronting the darkness head-on can we hope to banish it from our midst and restore purity and integrity to an industry that has long been tainted by the stain of evil.

Within the labyrinthine corridors of Hollywood, a nefarious presence looms large—the Luciferian managers and handlers who wield power like puppeteers, manipulating the destinies of artists with ruthless efficiency. David and I have delved deep into the shadowy realm of these enigmatic figures, uncovering the insidious methods by which they maintain control over the industry's elite.

Using blackmail and manipulation as their weapons of choice, these managers ensnare the unwary in a web of deceit and corruption from which escape seems impossible. Behind the facade of glitz and glamor, lies a world where loyalty is bought and sold, and where the pursuit of success comes at a steep price.

Through our research, we have shed light on the darker side of fame and fortune in Hollywood, revealing the sinister underbelly that lurks beneath the surface. The stories of artists who have fallen prey to the machinations of these Luciferian handlers serve as a chilling reminder of the dangers that lurk within the industry.

But even as we expose the truth of these manipulative tactics, we are keenly aware that the battle is far from over. For as long as there are those who are willing to sacrifice their integrity for the promise of fame and fortune, the grip of these Luciferian managers will remain unyielding.

Yet, in the face of adversity, there is hope. Through our continued efforts to shine a light into the darkest corners of Hollywood, we strive to empower artists to reclaim control over their own destinies and to break free from the chains of manipulation that bind them. For only by confronting the darkness head-on can we hope to bring about lasting change and restore integrity to an industry that has long been plagued by corruption and deceit.

In the murky depths of Hollywood's undercurrents, a chilling revelation emerges from David and my research—a revelation that shakes the very foundation of our understanding of the industry's dark secrets. It is the revelation of Lucifer's minions, malevolent entities that attach themselves to physical bodies in a desperate bid to experience life within the Earth realm.

Like parasites feeding on the souls of the vulnerable, these dark forces seek out unsuspecting individuals, latching onto them with an insatiable hunger for power and control. As if possessed by some unseen malevolence, they manipulate and exploit their hosts, driving them to unspeakable acts in the pursuit of their own twisted desires.

The implications of this revelation are staggering, suggesting a parasitic relationship between the dark forces that lurk in the shadows and the vulnerable individuals they seek to exploit. It is a relationship built on deception and manipulation, where the innocent are used as pawns in a sinister game of power and dominance.

As David and I delve deeper into the true extent of Lucifer's grip on the industry, the narrative of Hollywood's dark undercurrents becomes even more complex. We uncover stories of manipulation and exploitation that defy comprehension, shining a light on the insidious forces that lurk beneath the surface of glamor and fame.

But even as we confront the darkness head-on, we are reminded that the battle is far from over. For as long as there are vulnerable souls to prey upon, Lucifer's minions will continue to exert their influence, feeding off the innocence of those who dare to dream amidst the harsh reality of Tinseltown.

Yet, in the face of this darkness, there is hope. Through our research and our unwavering commitment to exposing the truth, we strive to empower individuals to break free from the grip of these malevolent entities and reclaim control over their own destinies. For only by confronting the darkness head-on can we hope to banish it from our midst and restore light to the heart of Hollywood.

The influence of Satanism in Hollywood serves as a sobering reminder of the dark underbelly that lurks within the entertainment industry. Through our research, David and I have unearthed unsettling truths that paint a disturbing picture of power and corruption, where the pursuit of wealth and fame comes at a steep and harrowing price.

From blood sacrifices performed by those in positions of great power to the insidious tactics of blackmail employed by Luciferian managers, the depths of depravity that exist within Hollywood are staggering. Behind the facade of glitz and glamor lies a world where morality is a fleeting concept, and where the pursuit of success often leads down a path of darkness and despair.

As the veil of illusion is lifted, it becomes painfully clear that Lucifer's grip on Hollywood extends far beyond the realm of fantasy, casting a long and ominous shadow over the glittering facade of Tinseltown. Beneath the surface lies a realm where the forces of good and evil wage an eternal struggle for supremacy, and where the innocent are all too often sacrificed on the altar of ambition.

But even in the face of such darkness, there is hope. Through our continued efforts to shine a light into the darkest corners of Hollywood, we strive to empower individuals to break free from the chains of manipulation and corruption that bind them. For only by confronting the truth head-on can we hope to banish the darkness from our midst and restore integrity to an industry that has long been tainted by the stain of evil.

As we continue our journey to uncover the secrets that lie within, let us not forget the importance of standing firm in the face of adversity. For though the road ahead may be long and fraught with peril, the light of truth will always prevail in the end, illuminating the path to redemption and righteousness for all who dare to seek it.

Understanding and Combating Sextortion and Revenge Porn

In the digital age, the prevalence of sextortion and revenge porn has become a distressing reality for many individuals, both young and old. These forms of exploitation not only invade personal privacy but also cause profound psychological and emotional harm. This chapter provides an in-depth understanding of these issues, their impacts, and the steps that can be taken by parents, guardians, educators, and law enforcement to protect and support those affected.

Sextortion is a form of exploitation where perpetrators threaten to release explicit images or videos of a victim unless the victim complies with their demands. These demands often include additional explicit material, money, or other favors. The crime leverages the victim's fear of humiliation and social ostracization, making them feel trapped and powerless.

Revenge porn involves the distribution of explicit images or videos of individuals without their consent, typically by someone seeking to humiliate or control them. This can affect anyone but is particularly prevalent among young adults and teenagers. The legal and social ramifications for victims can be devastating, resulting in emotional distress, reputational damage, and a deep sense of betrayal.

Children and adolescents are particularly vulnerable to sextortion. Offenders often use social media, gaming platforms, and other online spaces to approach minors. They manipulate their targets into sharing explicit content by pretending to be peers or trustworthy figures. Once the images are obtained, they threaten to distribute these to the child's family, friends, or school unless further demands are met.

The psychological impact on young victims can be severe. Many children experience overwhelming fear, shame, and helplessness. Tragically, some feel so trapped by their situation that they see no way out other than taking their own lives. This highlights the critical need for prompt and compassionate intervention.

While children are often the primary targets, adults are not immune to sextortion. Perpetrators exploit adults' personal and professional fears, threatening to send explicit content to colleagues, employers, or family members. The motivations remain the same—typically financial gain or further exploitation.

The emotional and psychological impact on adults can also be profound, leading to anxiety, depression, and even suicidal thoughts. The social and professional consequences can be equally damaging, affecting relationships and careers.

The accessibility of technology and the anonymity it can provide make it easier for predators to exploit their victims. Social media platforms, messaging apps, and even online games can be used to initiate contact and build a deceptive sense of trust. Predators meticulously groom their victims, slowly steering conversations towards sexual topics and requests for explicit material.

Parents and guardians should maintain open lines of communication with their children about online safety and the potential dangers of sharing personal information or images online. Discuss the tactics used by online predators and emphasize the importance of not engaging in conversations with strangers. Educate children about the dangers of sextortion and revenge porn. Use age-appropriate language to explain these concepts and provide practical advice on how to respond to suspicious or uncomfortable interactions. Use parental control tools to monitor children's online activities. This includes their social media interactions, messaging apps, and gaming platforms. Be aware of the websites and apps your children are using and who they are communicating with. Empower children to report any uncomfortable or threatening interactions to a trusted adult immediately. Reinforce that they will not be punished or blamed for coming forward.

It is crucial to keep all messages and evidence. Take screenshots, save chat transcripts, and ensure they are backed up on another device. This evidence can be vital for law enforcement investigations. Immediately contact local law enforcement or cyber tip lines. Organizations like the National Center for Missing & Exploited Children (NCMEC) can provide support and guidance. Psychological support for the victim is essential. Counseling can help manage the trauma and emotional fallout from such incidents. Many jurisdictions have laws against sextortion and revenge porn. Legal action can be pursued to hold perpetrators accountable. Familiarize yourself with the laws in your area and seek legal advice if necessary.

Educators and community leaders play a pivotal role in prevention and intervention. Schools should incorporate digital literacy and online safety into their curricula. Community organizations can host workshops and seminars for parents and children, raising awareness and providing practical advice.

Grooming is the process by which predators build trust with their victims, often over extended periods. They exploit this trust to manipulate children into engaging in sexual activities or sending explicit content. The anonymity of the internet allows predators to masquerade as peers or trusted adults.

Key indicators of grooming Extreme secrecy about internet activity. Unexpected presents or money. Withdrawal from family and friends. A sudden shift in behavior or emotion.

One notable example of an effective public service announcement is the video "Oblivious," created by a college senior. This video depicts the story of a young girl who receives a cell phone for her birthday and is subsequently groomed by an online predator. The video serves as a powerful educational tool, illustrating the dangers of online predators and the importance of vigilance and communication.

Sextortion and revenge porn are pervasive issues that require a concerted effort from parents, educators, law enforcement, and the community to combat. By fostering open communication, educating about online safety, and providing support to victims, we can protect our children and vulnerable adults from these devastating crimes. The fight against sextortion and online exploitation is ongoing, but with vigilance and collective action, we can make a significant impact.

Crisis in Law Enforcement and Child Safety Police and the Occult

In recent years, child safety specialists and law enforcement authorities throughout America have reported feeling overwhelmed by the sheer number of instances and complaints received daily. Whether the reports arrive through task forces, tip lines, or cyber tip lines, the consensus among these professionals is clear: there aren't enough hours to handle the influx of cases effectively. Despite a r bust framework of laws designed to protect children, the system is faltering under the weight of its responsibilities.

A significant component of the challenge is the requirement for more resources. Law enforcement agencies are often overburdened and need assistance properly prioritizing and investigating cases. Officers frequently express frustration over the inadequate support and time available to process cases thoroughly. This sense of being ill-equipped is compounded by many reports of sitting unattended on desks for weeks, with some even needing to be noticed entirely.

The public perception mirrors this internal frustration. Despite its legal foundations, there is a growing belief that the system needs to be fixed as effectively as it should. The reality is stark: laws alone are not enough. Implementation and enforcement require workforce, resources, and technology, all of which are in short supply.

The issue is further exacerbated by police departments' defunding and the ongoing struggles with recruiting new officers and staff. Even as the number of nonprofits and support groups across the United States grows, more efforts are needed to bridge the gap left by under-resourced law enforcement agencies. The collaborative approach involving non-profits, forensic interviewers, and various task forces is essential, but it often feels like a losing battle against an ever-growing tide of cases.

One glaring deficiency is the need for more specialized training within law enforcement. Back in 201, only 12% of law enforcement officers nationwide had received any training in human trafficking. By 2024, my estimates suggest that this figure has risen between 24% and 26%. While this increase is a positive development, it still leaves a significant portion of law enforcement needing more expertise to handle such cases effectively.

As society grapples with the rise in human trafficking, child abuse, and Internet safety concerns, it becomes evident that merely having trained officers is not enough. There must be an investment in resources, technology, and intelligence to support law enforcement efforts. Unfortunately, despite the prevalence of the "see something, say something" movement, many reports from vigilant citizens are brushed aside due to the overwhelming state of law enforcement agencies.

The quick speed of technical innovation, the proliferation of mobile phones, and the immediate distribution of information on social media means that the public is more interested than ever in reporting suspicious activity. However, the lag in law enforcement's response times often renders these timely reports less effective. This delay can be critical, as precious time is lost that could otherwise prevent further harm.

Fostering better collaboration between communities and law enforcement is imperative to address these challenges. Encouraging citizens to police their communities and engage in outreach efforts is a step in the right direction. However, the cycle of frustration and inefficiency will only continue with a corresponding increase in law enforcement's capacity to act on these reports.

In the coming years, finding solutions to streamline the reporting process and enhance investigative capabilities will be crucial. This includes ensuring that officers receive the necessary training and resources to respond swiftly and effectively to reports of child abuse and human trafficking. The system can become more responsive and efficient by leveraging technology and fostering stronger partnerships between law enforcement and community organizations.

The current state of child safety and law enforcement in America reflects a system under duress. While the dication of law enforcement officers and non-profit organizations is undeniable, their challenges are significant. Addressing these difficulties will require a coordinated effort to provide the appropriate resources, training, and technological assistance to guarantee that each report gets the attention it deserves. Such comprehensive measures can only create a safer environment for our children and a more effective law enforcement system.

The complex and often controversial relationship between law enforcement agencies and the investigation of crimes related to occult practices presents unique challenges. This chapter delves into historical and contemporary cases, the training and preparedness of law enforcement officers, the influence of media and public perception, and the delicate balance between protecting civil liberties and ensuring public safety. Understanding these facets provides a comprehensive view of how police pursue occult-related crimes and the broader implications for society.

The late 20th century witnessed a significant surge in public concern over alleged Satanic rituals and occult practices, a period often referred to as the "Satanic Panic." This era saw numerous high-profile cases where law enforcement agencies were called to investigate claims of ritualistic abuse and murder. These investigations were often fueled by media sensationalism and public fear, leading to widespread moral panic. A notable example is the McMartin preschool trial, where allegations of ritual abuse led to one of the longest and most expensive criminal trials in American history, ultimately resulting in no convictions.

Even before the Satanic Panic, law enforcement had sporadic encounters with crimes linked to occult practices. Historical cases of witch hunts, such as the Salem witch trials, reflect societal fear of the occult and the drastic measures taken to suppress it. These historical precedents set a tone of suspicion and often irrational fear that continues to influence contemporary policing practices.

Modern law enforcement training on occult-related crimes varies significantly across different jurisdictions. While some departments have developed specialized training programs, many officers still lack the specific knowledge required to handle these cases effectively. Training often includes identifying signs of occult practices, understanding the cultural and religious context, and distinguishing between actual criminal activity and protected religious practices.

One of the primary challenges in training officers to handle occult-related cases is the lack of comprehensive and standardized training materials. Furthermore, there is often a fine line between investigating potential crimes and infringing on religious freedoms. This balance is crucial in ensuring that investigations are both thorough and respectful of individuals' rights.

Media plays a significant role in shaping public perception of the occult and law enforcement's response to it. Sensationalist reporting can amplify fear and hysteria, leading to increased pressure on law enforcement agencies to act swiftly and decisively. This dynamic was particularly evident during the Satanic Panic, where media coverage often outpaced the evidence, leading to public outcry and demands for action.

Public perception of the occult and its associated risks can vary widely. In some communities, there is a deep-seated fear and mistrust of anything related to the occult, often influenced by cultural or religious beliefs. In others, there is a more nuanced understanding that distinguishes between harmless cultural practices and criminal activities. Law enforcement must navigate these differing perceptions to effectively manage investigations and maintain public trust.

Investigating crimes related to the occult requires a careful balance between protecting civil liberties and ensuring public safety. Law enforcement must be vigilant in respecting individuals' rights to freedom of religion and expression, even as they investigate potential criminal activities. Missteps in this area can lead to accusations of religious persecution and violations of constitutional rights.

At the same time, law enforcement has a duty to protect the public from harm. This includes investigating and prosecuting crimes that may be linked to occult practices, such as ritualistic abuse or murder. Effective policing in this area requires a clear understanding of the difference between protected religious practices and criminal activities that pose a genuine threat to public safety.

The advent of the digital age has transformed how occult practices are conducted and investigated. Online platforms have become hubs for various occult communities, facilitating both harmless cultural exchanges and, potentially, criminal activities. Law enforcement agencies now face the challenge of monitoring and investigating digital spaces without infringing on privacy rights.

Effective investigation of occult-related crimes often requires collaboration between different law enforcement agencies, including local police, federal agencies, and specialized task forces. Coordinating these efforts can be complex, particularly when cases cross jurisdictional boundaries or involve international elements.

One of the most notable contemporary cases involving allegations of occult-related crimes is that of the West Memphis Three. In 1993, three teenagers were convicted of the brutal murder of three young boys in West Memphis, Arkansas. The prosecution argued that the murders were part of a Satanic ritual, a claim that was later widely discredited. The case highlights the dangers of allowing public hysteria and inadequate evidence to drive criminal investigations.

Another intriguing but controversial series of cases involves the so-called "Smiley Face Killers." Some investigators believe that a series of drownings across the United States is the work of an organized group with occult connections. However, these claims remain unproven, and the cases continue to spark debate among law enforcement and the public.

The pursuit of Satan and the investigation of occult-related crimes present a unique set of challenges for law enforcement. Balancing the need to protect public safety with the imperative to respect civil liberties requires careful training, thoughtful policies, and ongoing dialogue between law enforcement and the communities they serve. As society continues to evolve and new technologies emerge, law enforcement must adapt to effectively manage the complexities of policing the occult while maintaining the trust and confidence of the public.

This chapter has explored the historical context, training challenges, media influence, and public perception issues surrounding law enforcement's relationship with the occult. Through examining case studies and contemporary challenges, it becomes evident that a nuanced approach is essential for navigating this complex landscape. Law enforcement must continuously evolve to meet these challenges, ensuring that investigations are thorough, respectful, and grounded in factual evidence to maintain public trust and safety.

The West Memphis Three: Unraveling the Mystery

The case of the West Memphis Three is one of the most controversial and widely debated criminal cases in recent American history. It involves the brutal murders of three eight-year-old boys in West Memphis, Arkansas, in 1993, and the subsequent arrest and conviction of three local teenagers. This chapter explores the details of the murders, the suspects, the investigations, the trials, and the theories surrounding the involvement of notorious criminal Edward Wayne Edwards.

On May 5, 1993, the small town of West Memphis, Arkansas, was thrust into turmoil when three eight-year-old boys—Stevie Branch, Michael Moore, and Christopher Byers—failed to return home after a day of playing. The boys were last seen together in the early evening, riding their bicycles around their neighborhood, which bordered the Robin Hood Hills, a patch of dense woods frequently used as a playground by local children.

When the boys did not come home, their parents grew increasingly anxious. Dana Moore, the mother of Michael, reported her son missing around 8:00 PM. Soon after, Pam Hobbs, Stevie's mother, and Melissa Byers, Christopher's mother, also reported their sons missing. A frantic search ensued, involving the boys' families, neighbors, and local police. They scoured the neighborhood and the nearby woods late into the night but found no trace of the children.

The following day, May 6, 1993, the search intensified. Around

1:45 PM, a juvenile parole officer, Steve Jones, discovered a child's shoe floating in a muddy creek that led to a drainage ditch in Robin Hood Hills. This grim find prompted further investigation of the area. Shortly after, the bodies of Stevie Branch, Michael Moore, and Christopher Byers were discovered submerged in the creek, naked and hogtied with their own shoelaces. Their clothing was found in the creek, some items of which were turned inside out, and had been weighed down with sticks.

The crime scene was appalling and suggested a horrific level of violence. The boys had been brutally beaten, and their bodies bore numerous injuries:

Stevie Branch: He had lacerations and contusions, consistent with being struck repeatedly. There were also signs of sexual mutilation.

Michael Moore: His injuries included severe head trauma, lacerations, and contusions. He too showed signs of having been beaten extensively.

Christopher Byers: His body exhibited the most severe mutilations. In addition to the beating and lacerations, he had been castrated. The autopsy revealed that his genitals had been partially removed, which fueled the theory of a ritualistic element to the murders.

The state of the bodies and the crime scene initially led investigators to consider the possibility of a ritualistic killing, particularly in the context of the Satanic Panic that was prevalent during the early 1990s. This hypothesis was further fueled by the brutal nature of the murders and the apparent precision of the mutilations.

The autopsies were conducted by the Arkansas State Crime Lab. The reports confirmed that all three boys had suffered multiple injuries before their deaths. The primary cause of death for Stevie Branch and Michael Moore was determined to be "multiple injuries." For Christopher Byers, it was "multiple injuries with sexual mutilation." The coroner estimated that the boys had died between the late evening of May 5 and the early morning of May 6.

The examination of the bodies revealed that the boys had been tied with their own shoelaces in a specific manner: their right wrists were tied to their right ankles, and their left wrists to their left ankles. This method of restraint suggested that the perpetrator(s) had taken time and care in binding the victims, adding to the horror and complexity of the case.

The discovery of the bodies sent shockwaves through the tight-knit community of West Memphis. The heinous nature of the crime led to widespread fear and outrage. The initial theory of a ritualistic killing was bolstered by the cultural context of the time, where there was significant public fear of satanic cults and ritual abuse.

Media coverage was intense, and the pressure on local law enforcement to solve the case quickly was immense. The brutal and seemingly senseless murders of three innocent children demanded swift justice, and the police were under significant scrutiny to find the perpetrators.

The tragic deaths of Stevie Branch, Michael Moore, and Christopher Byers marked the beginning of a long and convoluted journey for justice. The initial stages of the investigation set the stage for what would become one of the most controversial and hotly debated criminal cases in recent history. The brutal nature of the murders, combined with the social and cultural context of the early 1990s, led to a series of decisions and actions that would ultimately result in the wrongful convictions of the West Memphis Three and a continued quest for the truth.

The investigation into the murders in West Memphis was both swift and intense, driven by the shocking nature of the crime and the immense pressure on the West Memphis Police Department to solve the case quickly. Early on, the focus turned to the possibility of satanic ritual abuse, a direction heavily influenced by the broader societal context of the Satanic Panic era.

When the bodies of the three young boys were discovered, the police response was immediate. The crime scene was horrific, with the victims found in a drainage ditch, bound and mutilated. Given the brutality of the murders, law enforcement quickly mobilized all available resources. The West Memphis Police Department, aided by various local and state agencies, began an exhaustive search for clues and suspects.

The early 1990s were marked by widespread fear of satanic cults and ritualistic crimes. This period, known as the Satanic Panic, saw numerous allegations of satanic ritual abuse across the United States, often unsupported by substantial evidence. Media coverage sensationalized these fears, contributing to a climate of moral panic.

Against this backdrop, the police in West Memphis were primed to see the murders through the lens of satanic ritual abuse. The brutality of the crime seemed to fit the narrative of occult violence that was prevalent in the media and public discourse. This societal context heavily influenced the direction of the investigation.

Early in the investigation, law enforcement focused on local teenagers who did not conform to societal norms, particularly those with an interest in heavy metal music, gothic culture, and the occult. Damien Echols, Jason Baldwin, and Jessie Misskelley Jr., collectively known as the West Memphis Three, quickly came under suspicion.

Damien Echols, in particular, was singled out due to his appearance and interests, which included wearing black clothing and reading about occult practices. This profile made him an ideal suspect in the eyes of investigators looking for signs of satanic involvement.

The pressure to solve the case led to intense and sometimes questionable investigative techniques. Jessie Misskelley Jr., a teenager with a low IQ, was subjected to a lengthy interrogation without his parents or an attorney present. After hours of questioning, he confessed to the murders, implicating Echols and Baldwin. However, his confession was riddled with inconsistencies and factual inaccuracies about the crime scene.

Despite these inconsistencies, Misskelley's confession was used to arrest and charge all three teenagers. The confession played into the prevailing narrative of satanic ritual abuse, reinforcing the investigators' belief in their guilt.

Media coverage of the case was pervasive and sensationalist. Reports emphasized the supposed satanic elements of the crime, further inflaming public fear and hysteria. This media portrayal influenced public perception, creating a climate where the community demanded swift justice and presumed the guilt of the accused based on their nonconformity to social norms.

The trials of the West Memphis Three were heavily influenced by the narrative of satanic panic. The prosecution presented the case as a ritualistic murder carried out by teenagers steeped in occult practices. Despite the lack of physical evidence directly linking the defendants to the crime scene, the jury convicted all three. Damien Echols received the death penalty, while Jason Baldwin and Jessie Misskelley Jr. were sentenced to life imprisonment.

Years later, re-evaluation of the case brought to light numerous flaws in the investigation and trial. Advances in forensic science, particularly DNA testing, failed to connect the West Memphis Three to the crime scene. Additionally, new evidence suggested that the confession obtained from Jessie Misskelley Jr. was coerced and unreliable.

In 2011, after nearly two decades of legal battles, the West Memphis Three were released from prison following an Alford plea, which allowed them to assert their innocence while acknowledging that the prosecution had enough evidence to convict them. This resolution highlighted the profound impact of societal fear and media influence on the justice system.

The investigation into the West Memphis murders exemplifies the profound challenges and pitfalls that can arise when law enforcement is swayed by public hysteria and sensationalist media. The case underscores the importance of objective, evidence-based policing and the dangers of allowing societal fears to drive investigative decisions. The story of the West Memphis Three serves as a cautionary tale, reminding law enforcement and the public of the critical need to uphold rigorous standards of justice, even in the face of intense pressure and moral panic.

The investigation into the West Memphis murders swiftly focused on three local teenagers: Damien Echols, Jason Baldwin, and Jessie Misskelley, Jr. Collectively, they became known as the West Memphis Three. The background and characteristics of each suspect contributed to their profiling and eventual prosecution.

Damien Echols, 18 years old at the time, was perceived by law enforcement as the ringleader of the group. Echols had a history of mental health issues, including depression and a penchant for dark, alternative culture. His interests in the occult, heavy metal music, and unconventional fashion choices made him a prime suspect in the eyes of investigators. The prevailing narrative of the Satanic Panic era heavily influenced this perception, as law enforcement and the community were quick to associate his lifestyle with the ritualistic nature of the murders.

Echols' distinctive appearance and behavior amplified suspicions, making him a central figure in the investigation.

Jason Baldwin, 16 years old, was a close friend of Echols. Unlike Echols, Baldwin had no criminal record and was known as a good student. His academic performance and lack of disciplinary issues contrasted sharply with the image painted by investigators. However, his close association with Echols made him a target of suspicion. Baldwin's loyalty to his friend and their frequent companionship meant that he was often seen alongside Echols, thereby implicating him by association. The absence of direct evidence linking Baldwin to the crime was overshadowed by his connection to Echols, leading to his eventual arrest and prosecution.

Jessie Misskelley Jr., 17 years old, was particularly vulnerable due to his intellectual disability, with an IQ of 72, placing him in the category of intellectual disability. Misskelley was subjected to a prolonged and intense interrogation without the presence of a lawyer or his parents. During this interrogation, he eventually confessed to the murders, a confession he later recanted. Misskelley's confession was riddled with inconsistencies and inaccuracies about the crime, raising serious questions about its validity. Despite these issues, the confession played a crucial role in the arrests and charges against the three teenagers. The circumstances of Misskelley's interrogation and subsequent confession highlighted significant concerns about the investigative methods employed by the police.

The broader societal context of the Satanic Panic played a pivotal role in the investigation and prosecution of the West Memphis Three. The era was characterized by widespread fear and moral panic over alleged satanic cults and ritualistic crimes, heavily influencing public perception and law enforcement practices. This climate of fear led to a heightened sense of urgency to solve the case, often at the expense of due process and thorough investigation.

The media's sensationalist coverage of the case further fueled public hysteria. Reports frequently emphasized the supposed satanic elements of the crime, creating a narrative that resonated with the fears of the time. This coverage not only shaped public opinion but also exerted pressure on law enforcement to act swiftly and decisively. The portrayal of the West Memphis Three as dangerous occultists was largely constructed by the media, reinforcing the investigators' focus on them despite the lack of concrete evidence.

The trials of Damien Echols, Jason Baldwin, and Jessie Misskelley Jr. were heavily influenced by the narrative of satanic ritual abuse. The prosecution presented a case built on the alleged occult motivations of the suspects, despite the absence of physical evidence directly linking them to the crime scene. The reliance on Misskelley's flawed confession and the portrayal of Echols' interest in the occult as indicative of guilt underscored the biases at play.

Echols was sentenced to death, while Baldwin and Misskelley received life sentences. The convictions were a stark example of how societal fear and media sensationalism can impact the justice system, leading to potentially wrongful convictions based on circumstantial evidence and public pressure.

Years of legal battles and advocacy efforts eventually brought to light the numerous flaws in the investigation and trial. Advances in forensic science, particularly DNA testing, failed to connect the West Memphis Three to the crime scene. Additionally, new evidence suggested that Misskelley's confession had been coerced and was unreliable.

In 2011, the West Memphis Three were released from prison following an Alford plea, which allowed them to assert their innocence while acknowledging that the prosecution had enough evidence to convict them. This resolution highlighted the profound impact of societal fear and media influence on the justice system, underscoring the need for objective and evidence-based policing.

The case of the West Memphis Three serves as a cautionary tale about the dangers of allowing public hysteria and sensationalist media coverage to drive criminal investigations. The intense focus on occult-related suspicions, fueled by the Satanic Panic, led to the wrongful prosecution of three teenagers based on tenuous evidence and coerced confessions. This chapter illustrates the critical importance of maintaining rigorous standards of justice and the need for law enforcement to resist societal pressures and biases in their pursuit of truth and justice.

The trials of the West Memphis Three were fraught with controversy and sensationalism, reflecting the intense public interest and fear surrounding the case. The prosecution's strategy relied heavily on Jessie Misskelley's confession, despite its inconsistencies and the questionable circumstances under which it was obtained. Additionally, the prosecution called on so-called "occult experts" whose testimony linked the murders to satanic rituals, further sensationalizing the case and biasing the jury against the defendants.

A cornerstone of the prosecution's case was the confession obtained from Jessie Misskelley Jr. Despite its numerous inconsistencies and factual inaccuracies, the confession was presented as a clear admission of guilt. Misskelley, who had an intellectual disability and was interrogated without legal representation or parental presence, provided a statement that aligned with the prosecution's theory of a satanic ritual killing. The defense argued that the confession was coerced and unreliable, but the jury placed significant weight on it.

The prosecution also relied on testimony from so-called "occult experts" who asserted that the murders bore the hallmarks of a satanic ritual. These experts pointed to Damien Echols' interest in the occult, his dark attire, and his alternative lifestyle as evidence of his involvement in the crime. This testimony played into the prevailing fears of the Satanic Panic era, painting a picture of the defendants as dangerous and malevolent figures involved in ritualistic practices.

The defense highlighted the glaring lack of physical evidence linking Damien Echols, Jason Baldwin, and Jessie Misskelley Jr. to the crime scene. There were no fingerprints, DNA, or other forensic evidence tying the three teenagers to the murders. The defense emphasized that the prosecution's case was built on circumstantial evidence and unreliable testimony, urging the jury to consider the absence of direct proof.

The defense also challenged the credibility of the prosecution's witnesses, particularly the so-called "occult experts." They argued that the testimony was based on speculation and cultural biases rather than solid forensic science. Additionally, the defense pointed out the inconsistencies in Misskelley's confession and argued that it had been coerced under duress.

Throughout the trials, media coverage was intense and often sensationalist. Reports frequently highlighted the alleged satanic elements of the case, reinforcing public fears and biases. This sensationalist portrayal influenced public perception, creating a climate where the defendants were presumed guilty based on their appearance and interests rather than the evidence.

In 1994, the jury delivered their verdicts: Damien Echols was sentenced to death, while Jason Baldwin and Jessie Misskelley Jr. were given life sentences without the possibility of parole. The gruesome nature of the crime and the portrayal of the defendants as involved in satanic rituals swayed the jury, despite the defense's efforts to highlight the lack of physical evidence and the dubious nature of the prosecution's case.

Years of legal battles followed the convictions, with numerous appeals and petitions for retrial. Advances in forensic science, particularly DNA testing, eventually revealed no physical evidence linking the West Memphis Three to the crime scene. Additionally, new evidence and testimonies cast further doubt on the validity of Misskelley's confession.

In 2011, the West Memphis Three were released from prison following an Alford plea, which allowed them to maintain their innocence while acknowledging that the prosecution had enough evidence to convict them. This resolution underscored the deep flaws in the investigation and prosecution, highlighting the impact of societal fears and media influence on the justice system.

The trials of the West Memphis Three exemplify the profound challenges and pitfalls of a justice system influenced by public hysteria and sensationalist media coverage. The reliance on coerced confessions, dubious expert testimony, and cultural biases resulted in the wrongful convictions of three young men. This chapter serves as a cautionary tale about the importance of rigorous, evidence-based legal proceedings and the need for the justice system to remain impartial and unaffected by societal pressures and moral panics.

Over the years, numerous inconsistencies and flaws in the case against the West Memphis Three came to light, significantly altering public perception and fueling efforts to secure their release.

In the early 2000s, advances in DNA testing provided a pivotal breakthrough in the case. Tests revealed that none of the genetic material found at the crime scene matched Damien Echols, Jason Baldwin, or Jessie Misskelley Jr. This critical finding cast serious doubt on their guilt, undermining the prosecution's case, which had already been criticized for its reliance on circumstantial evidence and coerced confessions.

Further scrutiny of the evidence led to the emergence of new expert testimony and the retraction of earlier statements. Notably, some witnesses admitted to being pressured or coerced by law enforcement into giving false testimony. This new evidence suggested not only that the West Memphis Three might be innocent but also that their original trials were marred by significant legal and procedural errors.

As these revelations came to light, a growing movement advocating for the release of the West Memphis Three gained momentum. High-profile advocates, including celebrities, filmmakers, and legal experts, brought national and international attention to the case. Documentaries such as "Paradise Lost: The Child Murders at Robin Hood Hills" played a crucial role in highlighting the miscarriage of justice, galvanizing public opinion and support for the trio.

Celebrities like Johnny Depp, Eddie Vedder, and Peter Jackson used their platforms to raise awareness and funds for the legal battle to exonerate the West Memphis Three. This advocacy was instrumental in sustaining public interest and pressure on the judicial system to reevaluate the case.

After years of legal battles, the efforts to secure a retrial or outright exoneration culminated in 2011. Faced with mounting evidence of their potential innocence and the significant flaws in the original investigation and prosecution, the state offered a compromise: the Alford plea.

An Alford plea allows defendants to assert their innocence while acknowledging that the prosecution has enough evidence to convict them. For the West Memphis Three, accepting this plea was a pragmatic decision. It provided immediate release from prison while still allowing the state to avoid a full admission of wrongful conviction.

On August 19, 2011, Damien Echols, Jason Baldwin, and Jessie Misskelley Jr. entered Alford pleas and were subsequently released from prison. However, despite their freedom, they remained convicted felons, a status that continued to carry significant legal and social ramifications.

The case of the West Memphis Three continues to resonate as a powerful example of the potential for miscarriages of justice in the face of societal panic and media sensationalism. It highlights the importance of rigorous, evidence-based legal processes and the need for continual reassessment of past convictions in light of new evidence and advancements in forensic science.

The advocacy and public support that played such a crucial role in the eventual release of the West Memphis Three also underscore the impact that sustained public interest and activism can have on the justice system. The case has inspired ongoing efforts to reform legal procedures and ensure greater protections against wrongful convictions.

The post-conviction developments in the case of the West Memphis Three reflect a complex interplay of legal, social, and media influences. The advances in DNA testing and the retraction of dubious testimonies were critical in revealing the flaws in the original convictions. The sustained public advocacy, fueled by high-profile supporters and compelling documentaries, played an essential role in challenging the injustice faced by Echols, Baldwin, and Misskelley. While their release via Alford pleas marked a significant victory, the fact that they remain convicted felons serves as a reminder of the ongoing challenges in rectifying wrongful convictions and ensuring justice in the face of societal and systemic pressures.

The question of who truly committed the murders of the three young boys in West Memphis remains a topic of debate and speculation. Over the years, various theories have emerged, one of which involves Edward Wayne Edwards, a notorious criminal linked to several high-profile murders across the United States.

Edward Wayne Edwards was a career criminal and serial killer who managed to evade capture for decades. Born in 1933, Edwards' criminal activities spanned from the 1950s to the 2000s. He was finally apprehended in 2009 and later confessed to multiple murders. Edwards was known for his cunning ability to frame others for his crimes, adding a layer of complexity and deception to his already notorious criminal profile.

Edwards' criminal career was marked by a series of violent and often ritualistic murders. He had a penchant for staging crime scenes to mislead investigators, creating narratives that pointed suspicion away from himself and often towards innocent individuals. This behavior established him as a particularly elusive and dangerous offender, capable of manipulating evidence and exploiting weaknesses in the criminal justice system.

Some theorists believe that Edwards could have been involved in the West Memphis murders, given his history of committing ritualistic and staged killings. Proponents of this theory point to several aspects of the case that align with Edwards' known patterns of behavior: The gruesome nature of the West Memphis murders, with signs that could be interpreted as ritualistic, aligns with Edwards' modus operandi. He had a documented history of creating crime scenes that suggested ritualistic activity, often to throw off investigators. Edwards was notorious for framing others for his crimes. The controversial conviction of the West Memphis Three, based on questionable evidence and coerced confessions, fits the pattern of Edwards' tactics. The wrongful conviction of innocent parties could be seen as consistent with Edwards' established methods. Edwards was active during the period of the West Memphis murders and was known to travel extensively across the United States. This makes it plausible, though not proven, that he could have been in the vicinity of West Memphis at the time of the murders.

Despite these intriguing connections, there is no concrete evidence linking Edwards directly to the crime scene in West Memphis. The theory remains speculative, primarily driven by circumstantial correlations between Edwards' known behaviors and the peculiarities of the West Memphis case. No physical evidence has been found that ties Edwards to the West Memphis crime scene. Without DNA, fingerprints, or other forensic links, the theory lacks the hard evidence necessary to be taken as fact. Much of the theory is built on the patterns of Edwards' previous crimes rather than direct involvement. While the similarities are compelling, they are not definitive proof of his involvement in the

West Memphis murders. The absence of conclusive evidence against the West Memphis Three does not automatically implicate Edwards. There are other potential explanations and suspects that need to be considered, each requiring thorough investigation.

The theory involving Edward Wayne Edwards as a potential suspect in the West Memphis murders adds a layer of intrigue to an already complex and controversial case. While the connections to Edwards' criminal patterns provide an interesting angle, the lack of concrete evidence means this theory remains speculative. The debate over who truly committed the murders underscores the need for ongoing investigation and the importance of a justice system that is thorough, impartial, and evidence-based.

The involvement of Edwards, or lack thereof, does not detract from the broader issues highlighted by the West Memphis Three case, including the dangers of moral panic, the influence of media sensationalism, and the critical importance of ensuring that convictions are based on solid, irrefutable evidence.

The case of the West Memphis Three stands as a stark example of how fear, sensationalism, and flawed legal processes can lead to wrongful convictions. Despite their release, Damien Echols, Jason Baldwin, and Jessie Misskelley Jr. continue to fight to clear their names completely. The enduring mystery of who truly killed Stevie Branch, Michael Moore, and Christopher Byers remains unsolved, leaving a dark shadow over the justice system in West Memphis.

The case underscores the importance of rigorous standards in criminal investigations and the dangers of allowing public hysteria to influence the pursuit of justice. The reliance on coerced confessions, dubious expert testimony, and the influence of the media created a perfect storm that led to the conviction of three innocent teenagers. This tragic miscarriage of justice highlights several key lessons:

Criminal cases must be built on solid, irrefutable evidence. The lack of physical evidence linking the West Memphis Three to the crime scene was a critical flaw that should have been a major red flag during the investigation and trial. The interrogation of Jessie Misskelley Jr., conducted without legal representation or parental presence, led to a coerced confession that was full of inconsistencies. Legal safeguards must be in place to protect vulnerable individuals during interrogations to prevent false confessions. Media sensationalism can significantly impact public perception and, by extension, the judicial process. The portrayal of the defendants as satanic cult members influenced the jury's decision, demonstrating the need for a judicial system that remains impartial and insulated from public and media pressure. The eventual release of the West Memphis Three was in large part due to sustained advocacy and public support. This case illustrates the power of public awareness and advocacy in addressing and rectifying wrongful convictions.

The theory involving Edward Wayne Edwards as a potential suspect adds an intriguing dimension to the case but remains speculative without concrete evidence. Regardless of whether Edwards was involved, the case highlights the broader issue of ensuring justice is served through thorough and unbiased investigations.

Despite their release, the West Memphis Three continue to fight to fully clear their names and overturn their convictions. The true perpetrator(s) of the murders of Stevie Branch, Michael Moore, and Christopher Byers remain unknown, leaving an open wound for the victims' families and the community.

The tragedy of the West Memphis Three serves as a reminder of the profound consequences that miscarriages of justice can have on individuals and communities. It underscores the need for a justice system that prioritizes truth, evidence, and fairness over expediency and public appeasement. As society moves forward, the lessons from this case should inform efforts to prevent similar injustices, ensuring that the legal system upholds the principles of justice and integrity for all.

A Comprehensive Approach to Child Safety and Development

David and I have always formed an effective research team. David's approach is practical and factual, grounded in meticulous and methodical analysis, and consistently backed by solid data and hard evidence. In contrast, I delve into the philosophical and abstract aspects, providing an intuitive and holistic perspective that balances David's rigor. Our complementary strengths enable us to explore complex issues with precision and depth.

Every 40 seconds, a child goes missing or is abducted in the United States. This translates to approximately 840,000 children reported missing each year. The FBI estimates that between 85 and 90 percent of these cases involve children. The National Center for Missing and Exploited Children (NCMEC) provides additional context, estimating that around 2,000 children disappear from amusement parks, including Disneyland and Walt Disney World, annually. Of the 260,000 children abducted each year, approximately 200,000 are taken by a parent or other family member, often amid bitter divorce or custody battles. Despite these staggering numbers, only 1 out of every 10,000 missing children is not found alive. Studies show that 99.8% of missing children in the USA are eventually recovered, highlighting a high probability of safe returns.

The "Stranger Danger" concept has long been a part of American consciousness. Originating in the 1960s and 1970s, this phrase was part of a public safety campaign to teach children to avoid strangers who might pose a threat. The focus was primarily on the dangers posed by unknown individuals who could potentially abduct or harm children.

However, as time passed, the emphasis on stranger danger waned, only to be revisited with renewed urgency in various forms. In the 1980s and 1990s, high-profile cases of child abduction and murder reignited public fear and led to the resurgence of the "Stranger Danger" campaign. This period saw the introduction of new safety measures, including increased public awareness, child safety education, and the establishment of organizations dedicated to finding and protecting missing children, such as the NCMEC.

In recent decades, another form of "Stranger Danger" emerged, driven by concerns over satanic ritual abuse and alleged networks of child exploitation. This period, often referred to as the "Satanic Panic," began in the 1980s and involved widespread fears that organized groups were engaging in ritualistic abuse of children. Despite a lack of concrete evidence to support these claims, the panic led to numerous investigations and a heightened sense of vigilance among parents and authorities.

David and I have approached this complex and often controversial topic with practical research and philosophical inquiry. David's methodical nature ensures we base our findings on verifiable facts and credible sources. At the same time, my broader perspective helps contextualize these issues within the larger framework of societal fears and moral panics.

Our work underscores the importance of understanding both the statistical realities and the cultural narratives surrounding child abduction. By examining the data and the history of public perceptions, we aim to provide a comprehensive view of the phenomenon, helping to inform better protective measures and public awareness efforts.

Let's discuss the importance of positive attention in a child's development. Positive attention shapes a child's behavior, confidence, and overall well-being. By dedicating 10 minutes of undivided attention each day, you can notice significant improvements in your child's obedience and emotional growth. As parents, it's our responsibility to ensure our children receive the love and attention they need to thrive.

Positive attention can take many forms, including warmth, praise, interest, kindness, and quality time together. Effective communication, building on your child's strengths, and showing genuine interest in their activities can significantly reduce behavioral problems and create a strong bond between you and your child. Children who feel supported and loved develop confidence and are more likely to share their thoughts and experiences with you.

On the other hand, a lack of attention can lead to negative behaviors. Children might seek attention elsewhere, such as from peers or online, resulting in temper tantrums, arguing, and fighting. You create a secure environment where your child feels valued and understood by showing consistent positive attention through hugs, kisses, high fives, listening actively, making eye contact, and celebrating their successes.

In today's fast-paced world, it's easy to become overwhelmed by responsibilities. However, prioritizing your child's emotional needs is essential. When parents neglect to give their children attention, the streets, social media, and peer groups often fill the gap, sometimes with harmful consequences. Children who lack positive parental attention may be more vulnerable to negative influences and online dangers.

The online world, while offering many benefits, also poses significant risks. Ensuring your child's safety online is a daunting task, as the internet is rife with potential dangers, including predators. Parents must stay actively involved in their children's online activities. This consists of monitoring what they do online, having open and honest conversations about internet safety, and establishing trust and communication.

We hear too often in the news about teens falling victim to online predators. This reality should be a wake-up call for all parents. The odds may seem stacked against us, but we can protect our children by being vigilant and proactive. We must shift our focus back to the family, prioritizing our children's safety and well-being.

Teaching children how to use technology responsibly is part of this effort. Allowing them some freedom while providing oversight can help them learn to navigate the digital world safely. It's about balancing giving them space to grow and ensuring their safety. Building strong, trusting relationships with our children is vital. Everything matters—every interaction, every moment of attention. By staying involved and showing genuine care, we can guide our children through the complexities of today's world.

Positive attention is vital for a child's development. It fosters a sense of love, security, and confidence, reducing behavioral problems and strengthening the parent-child bond. In our fast-paced, technology-driven world, it's more important than ever for parents to be actively involved in their children's offline and online lives. By prioritizing positive attention and open communication, we can help our children grow into kind, confident, and well-adjusted individuals.

Mama's Sack Lunches
Conversation with David
and Me Breakfasts

Amidst the comforting ambiance of Mama's Sack Lunches, a quaint local eatery we frequent weekly, we were engrossed in deep conversation while working on our latest book. Nestled in the heart of our community, Mama's Sack Lunches serves delicious food and embodies the spirit of giving back, a value we deeply admire. As we wrapped up our meal and bid farewell to the friendly staff, I couldn't shake the thought of our discussion—it held the potential for an intriguing chapter.

Reflecting on our dialogue, I was inspired to delve into a captivating topic: the covert operation surrounding the creation of Satanic Super Soldiers. This enigmatic endeavor, blending elements of conspiracy theory, spiritual warfare, and apocalyptic prophecy, fascinated and unsettled us equally.

Returning home, I felt compelled to capture the essence of our conversation in writing, penning a chapter that peels back the layers of secrecy shrouding this covert program. It's a journey into the unknown, exploring the depths of human capability and the murky intersection of faith, fear, and foreboding prophecy.

The central theme of this chapter revolves around the orchestrated effort to create an army of "satanic super soldiers." These individuals are purportedly programmed through ritual abuse and mind control techniques to act as sleeper agents, waiting to be activated to bring about chaos and destruction. The idea is both alarming and intriguing, drawing parallels to the darker corners of psychological manipulation and spiritual warfare.

These super soldiers are described as being under the control of demonic forces, possessing extraordinary physical and mental capabilities due to their supernatural conditioning. The methodologies of mind control, including trauma-based conditioning and ritual abuse, are explored in detail. These methods are used to fracture the psyche of individuals, creating multiple personalities that can be triggered for specific purposes.

A significant portion of this chapter delves into the concept of spiritual warfare. It emphasizes the battle between good and evil, providing spiritual protection and combat strategies. Believers are urged to strengthen their faith and utilize spiritual tools such as prayer and scripture to resist demonic influences. The rise of these satanic super soldiers is presented as a sign of the approaching apocalypse, as foretold in biblical prophecies.

The chapter interprets contemporary events and societal changes as indicators of this impending chaos, urging readers to be vigilant and prepared for spiritual and physical battles. This interpretation serves as a call to action for those who believe in the power of faith and the importance of spiritual preparedness.

In our examination of historical precedents for mind control and ritual abuse, we delve deep into the murky waters of government projects like MK-Ultra. These covert operations, often veiled in secrecy, serve as harrowing reminders of the extent to which human experimentation can descend. By scrutinizing these past endeavors, we uncover disturbing parallels with the alleged creation of satanic super soldiers, shedding light on the eerie techniques purportedly employed by covert operations.

Drawing upon the dark history of MK-Ultra and similar projects, we reveal the chilling reality of psychological manipulation and trauma-based conditioning. The utilization of mind-altering substances, sensory deprivation, and other nefarious methods serves as a stark testament to the depths of human depravity when unchecked power and unethical experimentation intersect.

Moreover, by juxtaposing the methodologies of MK-Ultra with the alleged practices behind the creation of satanic super soldiers, we unveil unsettling similarities. The fragmentation of the psyche, the induction of multiple personalities, and the exploitation of vulnerable individuals echo across the annals of history, casting a shadow of doubt upon the moral integrity of those in positions of authority.

These historical references provide invaluable context and lend credibility to the narrative at hand. They serve as cautionary tales, warning us of the potential dangers lurking within the realm of human experimentation. By confronting the dark truths of our past, we are compelled to reckon with the possibility that such manipulative tactics may still be employed today, hidden beneath layers of secrecy and deception.

In shedding light on these historical precedents and parallels, we invite readers to critically examine the intersection of power, control, and ethical responsibility. It is a sobering reminder that the quest for knowledge must always be tempered by compassion, integrity, and respect for the inherent dignity of every human being.

World of human trafficking, drawing parallels to the sensational narrative of satanic super soldiers to underscore the gravity of the issue. It meticulously unpacks the complex machinery that drives trafficking operations, exposing the intricate web of facilitators, from recruiters to transporters to buyers.

The narrative underscores the staggering scope of the human trafficking industry, which rakes in billions of dollars annually. It emphasizes how this lucrative trade spares no corner of the globe, infiltrating even the most affluent and seemingly secure societies, including the United States.

Within this dark landscape, the chapter shines a spotlight on the particularly tragic plight of child trafficking victims. It meticulously explores how children, often the most vulnerable members of society, are systematically targeted, groomed, and exploited for various nefarious purposes. These include forced labor in sweatshops or agricultural fields, sexual exploitation in brothels or pornography rings, and even coercion into becoming child soldiers in conflict zones.

Moreover, the chapter doesn't shy away from detailing the chilling methods traffickers employ to trap and control their young victims. It delves into the tactics of deception, manipulation, and outright violence used to break their spirits and maintain control over them.

Efforts to combat human trafficking are portrayed as a daunting uphill battle but one that is vital to undertake. The chapter highlights the tireless work of law enforcement agencies, NGOs, and grassroots organizations in dismantling trafficking networks and providing support to survivors. Yet, it also acknowledges the need for a coordinated, global response to address the root causes of vulnerability that make individuals susceptible to exploitation in the first place.

In essence, this chapter serves as a sobering wake-up call, urging readers to confront the uncomfortable realities of human trafficking and to join the fight against modern-day slavery.

The role of technology and social media in facilitating trafficking is a significant theme. The chapter explains how these platforms make it easier for traffickers to find and groom their victims while also serving as tools for law enforcement and activists to track and combat trafficking networks. This dual role of technology is a crucial aspect of the modern trafficking landscape.

The efforts of law enforcement agencies to combat trafficking are discussed, highlighting the challenges they face, such as limited resources, corruption, and the complexity of international trafficking networks. The chapter critiques the legal frameworks in place, arguing that they often fall short of providing justice for victims and effectively dismantling trafficking operations.

Alarming statistics on human trafficking are presented, noting that millions of people are trafficked each year. Women and children are disproportionately affected, and the demand for cheap labor and commercial sex fuels the industry. By combining statistical analysis with personal stories and expert insights, this chapter brings to light the grim realities of human trafficking.

The various challenges in fighting trafficking are outlined, including jurisdictional issues, lack of international cooperation, and insufficient victim support services. The chapter advocates for a multi-faceted approach to address these challenges effectively. It underscores the importance of understanding both the statistical realities and the cultural narratives surrounding child abduction and trafficking.

With practical strategies aimed at fortifying themselves and their families against spiritual attacks. It delves into the fundamental pillars of spiritual protection: prayer, biblical study, and the support of a nurturing community within the church.

First and foremost, the chapter underscores the potency of prayer as a spiritual shield. It elucidates the importance of establishing a consistent and vibrant prayer life where individuals engage in intimate communion with the divine. Through prayer, they express their needs and desires and establish a direct line of communication with a higher power, drawing upon its strength and guidance to withstand spiritual onslaughts.

Moreover, the chapter delves into the transformative power of biblical study. It encourages readers to immerse themselves in the sacred texts, mining its depths for wisdom, insight, and spiritual nourishment. By grounding themselves in the timeless truths of scripture, individuals gain discernment to recognize and resist the snares of negative influences while also finding solace and encouragement in the promises and teachings of the Word.

Central to the discussion is the vital role of communal support within the church or spiritual community. Here, the chapter emphasizes fostering genuine, trusting relationships with fellow believers. Through collective worship, fellowship, and shared spiritual journey, individuals find strength in unity, support in times of trial, and accountability in their spiritual growth. This sense of belonging and interconnectedness is a formidable bulwark against spiritual attacks, as believers stand together in solidarity, offering mutual encouragement and protection.

Ultimately, the chapter advocates for a proactive approach to spiritual protection, urging readers to invest time and effort in cultivating these foundational practices. By prioritizing prayer, biblical study, and nurturing community ties, individuals and families can fortify themselves against spiritual assaults and navigate life's challenges with resilience, grace, and unwavering faith.

The Intersection of Satanic Super Soldiers and Human Trafficking" explores the intersection of mind control, spiritual warfare, and human trafficking. It passionately describes the unseen forces and strategies needed to combat them. This chapter aims to provide a comprehensive view of these complex issues, helping to inform better protective measures and public awareness efforts.

By examining the data and the history of public perceptions, this chapter underscores the importance of vigilance and preparedness in the face of these dark realities. It calls on readers to strengthen their faith, stay informed, and take an active role in protecting themselves and their loved ones from the pervasive threats of trafficking and spiritual warfare.

Criminal Networks, Pedophile Rings, and Serial Killers

The notion that organized crime and pedophile rings could intersect with the activities of serial killers is a chilling and complex hypothesis. This chapter delves into the potential connections between these nefarious entities, examining their sophistication, methods of operation, and the dark networks that may link them. By analyzing the strategies of luring victims, the disposal of bodies, and the evidence of interstate trafficking, we can explore the eerie parallels and possible collaborations among these criminals.

Organized crime syndicates and pedophile rings are known for their high levels of sophistication and organization. These groups often operate with a hierarchy, employ strict codes of conduct, and utilize advanced methods to evade law enforcement. Similar characteristics are found in the operations of some serial killers, particularly those who evade capture for extended periods.

For instance, serial killers like Ted Bundy and John Wayne Gacy demonstrated meticulous planning and an ability to blend into society, often mirroring the covert operations of organized crime. Bundy, with his charm and intelligence, and Gacy, with his respectable community standing, exemplify how these criminals can hide in plain sight. Similarly, organized crime figures employ legitimate businesses and social standing as fronts for illicit activities.

There are documented instances where serial killers have shown connections to broader criminal networks. The infamous case of Jeffrey Dahmer, who operated in Milwaukee, has speculated links to human trafficking rings due to the disappearance of several young men in the area during his killing spree. Additionally, Henry Lee Lucas and Ottis Toole claimed involvement in a network of killers, which, though primarily dismissed, points towards the possibility of such connections.

These claims, while often unreliable, suggest that the idea of serial killers operating within or alongside organized crime and pedophile rings is not entirely far-fetched. The overlap in victim profiles, operational methods, and geographic locations between these criminals may indicate more profound, more systematic collaborations.

Through our research and our boots on the ground, David and I found that there is often anecdotal evidence and whispers within communities that hint at these connections, though concrete proof is elusive.

Both serial killers and organized crime syndicates often employ cunning and manipulation to lure their victims. Serial killers like Bundy used their charm and a guise of vulnerability to attract victims. Pedophile rings, on the other hand, frequently exploit positions of trust or authority, such as coaching, teaching, or religious roles, to gain access to children.

Organized crime networks also utilize sophisticated recruitment and exploitation methods, sometimes through the promise of employment or better living conditions, which can overlap with tactics used by human traffickers. This similarity in methodology indicates a shared understanding of psychological manipulation and exploitation.

The disposal of bodies is another area where parallels between these groups are evident. Organized crime has long been associated with efficient and untraceable methods of disposing of bodies, often involving remote locations, incineration, or the use of industrial processes. Serial killers, particularly those who are highly organized, employ similar techniques to evade detection.

For example, Robert Pickton, who was convicted of the murder of numerous women in Canada, used his pig farm to dispose of bodies, a method reminiscent of organized crime's utilization of remote or industrial sites for body disposal. The sophistication of these methods suggests a possible exchange of knowledge or shared operational practices between different types of criminals.

Interstate trafficking is a common thread connecting organized crime, pedophile rings, and some serial killers. Criminal networks often span multiple states, utilizing a web of connections to traffic drugs, weapons, and humans. Serial killers like Israel Keyes, who traveled extensively across the United States to commit his crimes, demonstrate similar patterns of movement and operational reach.

These interstate activities complicate law enforcement efforts, as jurisdictional boundaries can hinder the sharing of information and coordination of resources. The ability of these criminals to operate across state lines points to a level of organization and resourcefulness that blurs the lines between different types of criminal activities.

Known criminal networks, such as the Mafia, have been implicated in various illegal activities, including human trafficking and drug distribution. These networks often intersect with other illicit enterprises, creating a complex web of criminal activity. Investigations have sometimes uncovered links between these networks and individuals involved in serial killings or pedophile rings.

For instance, the Franklin Scandal of the late 1980s implicated high-profile individuals and alleged connections between child abuse, trafficking, and organized crime. While many aspects of the case remain contentious and disputed, it highlights the potential for such connections and the difficulty in unraveling these deeply embedded networks.

The potential connections between organized crime, pedophile rings, and serial killers present a disturbing but necessary area of investigation. The similarities in their methods of operation, victim selection, and evasion tactics suggest a possible overlap or collaboration that complicates efforts to combat these crimes. Understanding these connections can provide critical insights for law enforcement and help develop more effective strategies to dismantle these dark and intertwined networks. By shedding light on these sophisticated and organized operations, we move closer to protecting vulnerable populations and bringing perpetrators to justice.

Norman, John David A Comprehensive Analysis

John David Norman is a notorious figure in the annals of American crime, primarily known for his extensive involvement in child molestation, child pornography, and sex trafficking. Spanning several decades, Norman's criminal activities and his alleged connections to infamous serial killers such as Dean Corll and John Wayne Gacy have left a dark stain on American history. This paper delves into Norman's life, his criminal enterprises, and the broader implications of his actions on society.

John David Norman's early life remains obscure, but his criminal activities began to surface in the 1960s. Convicted multiple times between 1960 and 1998, Norman's crimes predominantly involved child molestation and the production and distribution of child pornography. His repeated offenses highlight a persistent and dangerous pattern of behavior. Norman was the mastermind behind several notorious operations dedicated to child exploitation.

Based in Dallas, the Odyssey Foundation was one of Norman's initial ventures into the illicit world of child pornography. This direct mailing service was designed to distribute obscene material and facilitate the sex trafficking of minors. The Foundation's operations exposed the extent of Norman's reach and ability to evade law enforcement for years.

Norman's criminal activities expanded with the Delta Project, Creative Corps, and M-C Publications, all based in Chicago. These entities functioned similarly to the Odyssey Foundation, focusing on the distribution of child pornography and the organization of sex trafficking networks. Norman's operations in Chicago demonstrated a sophisticated and calculated approach to his criminal enterprises, using various front organizations to obscure his activities.

The Handy Andy operation in Pennsylvania marked another phase of Norman's extensive network. This venture continued the patterns seen in his previous enterprises, further entrenching Norman in the world of child exploitation. The persistence of these operations across different states underscores the systemic nature of Norman's crimes.

One of the most chilling aspects of John David Norman's criminal history is his alleged links to notorious serial killers Dean Corll and John Wayne Gacy.

Dean Corll, infamously known as the "Candy Man," terrorized Houston, Texas, in the early 1970s. His heinous acts resulted in the deaths of at least 28 boys and young men, often with the assistance of teenage accomplices David Brooks and Elmer Wayne Henley. Corll lured his victims with promises of parties and rides, only to subject them to horrific torture and murder.

The alleged connection between John David Norman and Dean Corll remains one of speculation rather than concrete evidence. Both individuals operated within the same dark underworld of child exploitation and sexual abuse, leading some investigators to hypothesize potential overlaps in their activities. Given the time frame and the nature of their crimes, it is plausible that they moved within similar criminal networks, possibly sharing contacts or resources.

John Wayne Gacy, also known as the "Killer Clown," was responsible for the deaths of at least 33 young men and boys in the Chicago area during the 1970s. Gacy's modus operandi involved luring his victims to his home under various pretenses before sexually assaulting and murdering them. The connection between Gacy and John David Norman is more tangible and disturbing, primarily facilitated through Norman's associate, Phillip Paske.

Phillip Paske's involvement in Norman's network and his subsequent connection to Gacy sheds light on a potential supply chain for Gacy's victims. Paske was reportedly responsible for procuring young boys for Gacy, which raises chilling questions about the extent of Norman's network and its potential role in feeding Gacy's murderous impulses.

Paske's relationship with Norman suggests that Norman's extensive child exploitation operations may have inadvertently, or perhaps knowingly, supplied victims to Gacy. This connection paints a broader and more sinister picture of the interconnectedness of pedophile rings and serial killings.

Understanding the connections between Norman, Corll, and Gacy necessitates an exploration of the nature of criminal networks involved in child exploitation and trafficking. These networks often operate in the shadows, with individuals and groups facilitating the movement and exploitation of children across state lines and even internationally.

The likelihood of Norman, Corll, and Gacy operating within similar criminal circles is high. These circles are typically composed of individuals who share common interests in exploiting children for sexual purposes. Such networks thrive on secrecy, mutual trust, and exchanging illicit materials and victims. The overlap between Norman's operations and the activities of Corll and Gacy suggests that these criminals might have shared resources, either directly or indirectly, enhancing their ability to perpetrate their crimes.

Norman's operations, including the Odyssey Foundation and the Delta Project, were structured to distribute child pornography and facilitate sex trafficking. These enterprises required a steady supply of new victims, which could have been obtained through various means, including the recruitment of runaways, abductions, and grooming. Phillip Paske's role as an intermediary indicates a more organized method of victim procurement and distribution, where individuals like Paske acted as brokers between suppliers and consumers of child exploitation.

The connections between Norman, Corll, and Gacy have given rise to numerous conspiracy theories and speculations. Some believe that a larger, more organized pedophile ring operated behind the scenes, with high-profile figures and organized crime elements involved. While concrete evidence supporting these theories remains limited, the persistent rumors highlight these criminal networks' complex and elusive nature.

Law enforcement agencies face significant challenges in dismantling such networks. The covert operations and the involvement of seemingly respectable individuals in society make detection and prosecution difficult. Norman's ability to evade capture for extended periods exemplifies the cunning and resourcefulness of such criminals.

The implications of these connections are profound for the victims and their families. The potential for victims to have been trafficked through such networks adds layers of trauma and complexity to their experiences. Understanding these connections is crucial for providing appropriate support and justice for the victims.

The alleged links between John David Norman, Dean Corll, and John Wayne Gacy underscore the sinister and interconnected nature of child exploitation and serial killings. While direct evidence is sparse, precise connections suggest a broader, more organized criminal enterprise. These connections highlight the need for continued vigilance, sophisticated investigative techniques, and comprehensive support systems for victims to combat the persistent and pervasive threat of child exploitation and trafficking.

Despite his extensive criminal activities, Norman's operations were often elusive to law enforcement. His ability to create and manage multiple front organizations across different states allowed him to evade capture for extended periods. However, Norman's luck eventually ran out, and he faced numerous convictions over the decades.

Norman's convictions between 1960 and 1998 highlight a career marred by repeated offenses and legal battles. Each conviction painted a clearer picture of a man deeply entrenched in criminal activities, showing little remorse or intention to reform. His sentences, though varied, underscored the seriousness of his crimes and his persistent threat to society.

The legacy of John David Norman is one of darkness and tragedy. His operations not only exploited countless children but also highlighted significant gaps in law enforcement's ability to combat child exploitation effectively. Norman's connections to high-profile serial killers further underscore the dangerous intersections of various criminal activities.

John David Norman remains a significant, though often overlooked, figure in the history of American crime. His life and activities provide crucial insights into the operations of child exploitation networks and the challenges faced by law enforcement in tackling such pervasive and hidden crimes. Understanding Norman's methods and connections is essential for developing better strategies to prevent and combat child exploitation in the future.

Herb Baumeister's Case A serial murderer was murdered at Fox Hollow Farm

Herb Baumeister stands as a chilling figure in the history of American serial killers, known for his predatory behavior and the gruesome discovery of remains on his property in the 1990s. Baumeister's life and crimes underscore the darkness lurking behind seemingly ordinary facades. This paper delves into the details of his crimes, the investigation that led to the discovery of his victims, and the broader implications of his actions.

Herb Baumeister, an ostensibly successful businessman from Indiana, became one of the most notorious serial killers in American history following the gruesome discovery of human remains on his property in the mid-1990s. This paper explores the details of the bodies found on Fox Hollow Farm, examines the conspiracies surrounding Baumeister's crimes, and investigates potential connections to other unsolved cases and criminal networks.

Herb Baumeister was born in Indianapolis, Indiana, on April 7, 1947. Social difficulties and increasingly bizarre behavior marked his early life. As a teenager, Baumeister exhibited troubling signs of mental illness, which later were believed to have included schizophrenia and dissociative identity disorder. Despite these issues, Baumeister managed to maintain a semblance of normalcy, attending Indiana University and later marrying his wife, Julie.

In the 1980s and early 1990s, Herb Baumeister achieved the American dream. He co-founded the successful thrift store chain Sav-A-Lot in Indianapolis and lived with his family in the affluent suburb of Westfield, Indiana. However, beneath this veneer of success lay a man harboring dark and murderous inclinations.

Baumeister's predatory behavior primarily targeted young men whom he would lure to his estate under the pretense of engaging in consensual sexual activity. His modus operandi often involved meeting his victims in gay bars in Indianapolis, where he would entice them with the promise of alcohol and drugs. Once they were at his property, Fox Hollow Farm, Baumeister would strangle his victims to death.

The investigation into Baumeister's crimes began in earnest in the mid-1990s, spurred by the persistent efforts of a private investigator hired by the family of a missing man. In June 1996, police obtained a search warrant for Fox Hollow Farm, leading to the discovery of approximately 10,000 skeletal fragments on the property. These remains were later identified as belonging to at least 11 men, though authorities suspected that Baumeister's victim count could be much higher, potentially spanning several states.

The forensic investigation at Fox Hollow Farm was a painstaking process. Due to the extensive decomposition and scattering of remains, identifying the victims and reconstructing the sequence of events was challenging. Anthropologists and forensic specialists worked meticulously to piece together the fragments, using dental records and DNA analysis to identify some of the victims.

Baumeister's case presented several legal and investigative challenges. Firstly, his ability to evade detection for so long highlighted significant gaps in communication and coordination among law enforcement agencies. Furthermore, Baumeister fled to Canada during the investigation and ultimately committed suicide before he could be apprehended, thereby avoiding prosecution and leaving many questions unanswered.

The victims of Herb Baumeister were primarily young men in their twenties, often from marginalized communities. Their disappearances went largely unnoticed due to the transient lifestyles many led. The emotional toll on the families of these victims was immense, exacerbated by the difficulty in identifying remains and the lack of closure due to Baumeister's suicide.

Analyzing Baumeister's psychological profile reveals a deeply disturbed individual. His double life—a respectable businessman and a sadistic murderer—demonstrates a high level of compartmentalization. Baumeister's actions suggest a combination of psychopathy and severe mental illness, driving his compulsive need to control and dominate his victims.

The Baumeister case has broader implications for understanding serial killers and improving investigative techniques. It highlights the need for better mental health interventions and more robust systems for tracking missing persons, particularly those from vulnerable populations. Additionally, it underscores the importance of inter-agency cooperation in solving complex criminal cases.

Herb Baumeister's crimes and the subsequent discovery of his victims' remains present a haunting narrative of a serial killer hidden in plain sight. The investigation into his actions brought justice to the victims and shed light on the complexities of tracking and apprehending serial offenders. The case remains critical in forensic science, criminal psychology, and law enforcement methodologies.

In the summer of 1996, the investigation into Baumeister's activities intensified following a tip from a private investigator. The police obtained a search warrant for Baumeister's property, Fox Hollow Farm, in Westfield, Indiana. While searching, investigators found thousands of human bone fragments scattered across the property. These remains were later confirmed to belong to at least 11 young men, although the actual number of victims could be significantly higher.

The forensic analysis of the remains was a complex and time-consuming process. Due to the extensive decomposition and scattering of bones, investigators faced challenges in identifying the victims. Forensic anthropologists and specialists employed various techniques, including dental record comparisons and DNA analysis, to piece together the identities of the deceased. Some remains were burned or otherwise disfigured, complicating the identification process.

One of the most persistent conspiracies surrounding Baumeister's crimes is the potential connection to other notorious serial killers operating during the same period. Some investigators and theorists suggest that Baumeister may have had ties to a more extensive network of killers, similar to the speculated connections between John Wayne Gacy and other criminals.

Baumeister was known to travel frequently between Indiana and Ohio, often visiting gay bars to find his victims. This has led to speculation that he might have committed murders outside of Indiana, contributing to the disappearance of men in other states. The lack of concrete evidence and Baumeister's suicide in 1996 have left many of these cases unresolved, fueling conspiracy theories about the true extent of his crimes.

Another theory posits that Baumeister could have been part of an organized crime syndicate or a pedophile ring. This theory is based on the sophisticated nature of his operations and the sheer number of victims. The presence of an elaborate network could explain how Baumeister managed to evade detection for so long and why his activities extended beyond the local area.

Herb Baumeister's gruesome activities at Fox Hollow Farm have sparked numerous theories and speculations. Among these is the possibility that Baumeister was involved in an organized crime syndicate or a pedophile ring. This theory suggests that his operations were far more sophisticated and extensive than initially perceived, potentially involving a broader network of criminals engaged in similar activities.

Several aspects of Baumeister's operations point to a level of sophistication that could imply involvement in a more extensive criminal network. Baumeister frequented gay bars in Indianapolis to find his victims, using charm and persuasion to lure them back to his property. His ability to consistently find and transport his victims without raising suspicion suggests a systematic approach. The discovery of approximately 10,000 skeletal fragments on his property indicates a systematic method of body disposal. The scattered and burned remains suggest an attempt to obscure the identities of his victims and hinder forensic analysis.

Baumeister's frequent travels between Indiana and Ohio, coupled with the potential links to other unsolved cases along Interstate 70, suggest a broader operational range than typically seen in lone serial killers. This mobility indicates a level of coordination and planning.

The theory that Baumeister was part of an organized crime syndicate or pedophile ring stems from the following considerations. Serial killers operating within a network often have accomplices who assist in various aspects of their crimes, from victim procurement to body disposal. The sophistication of Baumeister's methods implies possible assistance or knowledge from others involved in similar criminal activities. Pedophile rings operate by exploiting vulnerable children and young adults, often involving multiple perpetrators who share resources and victims. Baumeister's targeting of young men and the sheer number of his victims suggests he could have been part of such a ring, which would provide him with a steady supply of potential victims and methods for evading detection. Members of organized crime syndicates often benefit from protection and resources that help them evade law enforcement. Baumeister's ability to continue his activities without being caught could indicate that he had access to such resources, possibly through a more extensive criminal organization.

The case of John David Norman, a convicted pedophile with connections to other notorious criminals, provides a possible parallel to Baumeister's activities. Norman's extensive network for distributing child pornography and trafficking young boys shares similarities with the suspected scope of Baumeister's operations. The possibility that Baumeister was connected to similar networks cannot be overlooked.

The hypothesis that Baumeister was involved in interstate trafficking aligns with the pattern of disappearances and unsolved murders along major highways like Interstate 70. Organized crime syndicates often exploit such routes for illegal activities, including human trafficking and drug distribution. Baumeister's frequent travel and the location of some of his victims' remains suggest he might have been part of such a network.

One of the primary challenges in substantiating the theory of Baumeister's involvement in organized crime is the lack of direct evidence.

Baumeister's suicide in 1996 precluded any thorough interrogation that might have revealed connections to more extensive networks.

Law enforcement agencies often need help sharing information across jurisdictions, particularly in cases involving transient populations and interstate activities. This fragmentation can hinder the ability to piece together a comprehensive picture of Baumeister's potential connections.

The difficulty in identifying many of Baumeister's victims complicates efforts to trace their movements and potential links to other criminal activities. Without knowing who the victims were, it is challenging to determine whether they were part of a broader trafficking network.

If Baumeister were indeed part of an organized crime syndicate or pedophile ring, it would necessitate a broader investigation into similar networks operating in the region. This could potentially uncover other perpetrators and prevent future crimes.

Understanding Baumeister's possible connections to organized crime underscores the need for improved coordination and information sharing among law enforcement agencies. Enhanced collaboration could lead to more effective strategies for identifying and dismantling criminal networks.

Recognizing the potential involvement of organized crime in Baumeister's activities highlights the importance of providing comprehensive support for the victims and their families. This includes identifying and memorializing the victims and addressing the broader impact of such crimes on communities.

The theory that Herb Baumeister was part of an organized crime syndicate or pedophile ring adds a complex and sinister dimension to his already horrifying crimes. While concrete evidence remains elusive, the sophistication of his operations and the sheer number of victims suggest that his activities might have extended beyond the actions of a lone serial killer. Investigating these potential connections further could provide crucial insights into preventing similar atrocities and ensuring justice for the victims.

One of the more intriguing connections involves the "I-70 Strangler," a serial killer active in the early 1990s who targeted young men along Interstate 70 in Indiana and Ohio. The modus operandi of the I-70 Strangler closely mirrors that of Baumeister, leading some investigators to speculate that Baumeister might be responsible for these murders as well. However, this connection remains speculative due to the lack of definitive evidence linking him to these crimes.

Numerous missing persons cases from the Midwest during the 1980s and 1990s have been re-examined in light of Baumeister's crimes. Families of missing men who fit Baumeister's victim profile have urged law enforcement to revisit these cases, hoping for closure. While some connections have been made, many cases remain unsolved, leaving the possibility that Baumeister's accurate victim count is far higher than currently documented.

One significant challenge in investigating Baumeister's crimes was the need for coordination among law enforcement agencies across state lines. Baumeister's ability to operate undetected for so long highlights the need for better communication and data sharing between jurisdictions, particularly in cases involving transient populations and serial offenders.

Baumeister's psychological profile is crucial to understanding his actions and evading capture for so long. His ability to maintain a double life as a family man and successful businessman while committing heinous crimes demonstrates a high level of compartmentalization and deceit. Profilers believe that Baumeister exhibited traits of psychopathy, including a lack of empathy, manipulativeness, and a propensity for violent behavior.

The case of Herb Baumeister remains one of the most perplexing and horrifying in American criminal history. The discovery of numerous human remains on his property at Fox Hollow Farm unveiled a grim narrative of a serial killer operating in plain sight. The conspiracies and theories surrounding his crimes, including potential connections to other serial killers and unsolved cases, continue to intrigue and haunt investigators and the public alike.

Baumeister's case underscores the importance of thorough and coordinated investigative efforts, the need for advancements in forensic science, and the necessity of addressing the psychological underpinnings of such criminal behavior. As the true extent of Baumeister's crimes may never be fully known, his story is a cautionary tale about the darkness behind even the most benign exteriors.

David and I ramble and prepare for a podcast

David and I discussed doing a podcast about this topic, and when we finished discussing the show episode, we decided that this would be a chapter in our book.

In the digital age, the emergence of cyberbullying has introduced a new form of cruelty among youth. With keyboards as weapons, bullies have infiltrated homes, bringing harm to victims as surely as if they had entered with physical violence. The psychological torment inflicted is often gradual and relentless, filled with lies, rumors, and daily cruelty that can lead to devastating consequences, including teen suicide.

Cyberbullying is a significant issue that affects countless families across the United States. It triggers a cascade of problems, from emotional distress to severe mental health issues. As we delve into this topic, we'll explore cyberbullying, how it operates, its various forms, and, most importantly, what can be done to combat it.

Cyberbullying involves the use of digital technologies to harass, threaten, or humiliate someone. Unlike traditional bullying, cyberbullying can happen 24/7 and reach a person even when they are alone. It manifests in many ways, including Instant messaging, text messaging, and harassment via email and social media platforms. They are stealing passwords and altering victims' profiles with offensive content, sending harmful images or messages to intimidate or harass, and distributing viruses, spyware, and hacking programs to compromise the victim's digital security and creating sites specifically designed to insult or bully individuals and using these platforms to spread harmful rumors or engage in collective bullying. Cyberbullying is often a precursor to more severe issues like depression, anxiety, and, in extreme cases, suicide.

Peer pressure is another factor that significantly impacts youth, pushing them towards cyberbullying or other harmful behaviors. While peer influence can sometimes be positive, encouraging good habits and academic success, it often leads to adverse outcomes. Children may succumb to peer pressure due to a desire to fit in, fear of rejection, or simply out of curiosity.

Positive and Negative Aspects of Peer Pressure Friendships, positive examples, feedback, and advice. Stress, discomfort, and coercion into activities like drug use or cyberbullying.

Young people must trust their instincts, plan ahead for challenging situations, and learn to say no to handle peer pressure.

Addressing cyberbullying requires a comprehensive approach involving parents, educators, and community members. Victims should avoid replying to harmful messages but must keep a record of all communications. Incidents should be reported to schools, law enforcement, and online platforms. Parents should stay informed about their children's internet use and maintain open lines of communication. Schools and communities should implement programs to educate children about the dangers of cyberbullying and how to handle it. Safe spaces should be established where children can talk about their experiences and seek help.

It's vital to remember that asking for help is a sign of strength, not weakness. Numerous resources and organizations are available to support families and children affected by cyberbullying.

While the internet is a powerful tool, it can also be misused to harm children. Parents, educators, and community leaders must take collective action to protect young people. This involves monitoring online activity, providing educational resources, and fostering environments where children feel safe and supported.

We must prioritize education and awareness to combat cyberbullying effectively. By equipping our children with the knowledge and tools to navigate the digital world safely, we can reduce the incidence of cyberbullying and its devastating effects. It's not just a task for parents but a responsibility for the entire community, including schools, churches, and local organizations.

Human trafficking is a hidden yet pervasive issue affecting countless individuals across the globe. 2015 Racine County became painfully aware of this crisis when 35 victims were recovered. On January 31st, Great Lakes Church hosted a vigil to raise awareness and honor these victims. The event highlighted the insidious nature of human trafficking and its far-reaching consequences.

Simultaneous events in Racine County provided the public with essential resources to identify and support trafficking victims. Organized by the "Racine Coalition Against Human Trafficking," these gatherings aimed to educate the community and promote vigilance.

Karri Hemmig, the coalition's executive director, emphasized that human trafficking often goes unnoticed. Victims frequently appear to lead everyday lives, attending school and church, making it difficult to recognize their plight. Hemmig noted that human trafficking cases have been prosecuted in every Wisconsin county, but Racine's location between Milwaukee and Chicago along the I-94 corridor poses unique challenges. This area is a significant route for traffickers.

Traffickers often pose as boyfriends to manipulate young victims, sometimes as young as 11 or 12 years old. Eileen Geisler, who works closely with victims, shared her initial disbelief at the prevalence of trafficking in her town. Survivors at the vigil recounted their harrowing experiences, emphasizing the need for community awareness and intervention.

Community members should watch for indicators of trafficking, such as older men with young, timid girls or individuals carrying multiple cell phones. Experts estimate that in 2015, up to 500 children were trafficked for sex in the United States, underscoring the urgent need for action.

Jeremy Moore, a pastor at Great Lakes Church, highlighted the crucial role of faith communities in addressing human trafficking. He stressed the importance of support and prayers for victims, reinforcing that their lives have value and purpose despite their suffering.

The Wisconsin Attorney General's Office has established a coalition to combat sex trafficking. Increased reporting and proactive law enforcement efforts are crucial in identifying and prosecuting traffickers.

The events in Racine County underscored the importance of community engagement in the fight against human trafficking. By staying informed, vigilant, and supportive, residents can protect vulnerable individuals and bring traffickers to justice.

The rise of digital technology has introduced new risks for our children, from cyberbullying to exposure to harmful content. Parents, educators, and community leaders must unite in safeguarding our youth.

Children should be educated about internet safety, cyberbullying, and the importance of respectful online behavior from a young age. Parents must monitor their children's online activities, maintain open communication, and provide guidance on handling negative experiences.

Numerous resources, including government agencies and nonprofit organizations, are available to help families navigate these challenges. Communities must leverage these resources and create supportive environments where children can thrive.

Empowerment begins with education and open dialogue. By equipping children with the tools to make informed decisions and encouraging families to seek help, we can create a safer, more supportive environment for our youth.

In our fast-paced society, losing sight of the connection with our children is easy. However, the stakes are too high to ignore. By collectively addressing issues like cyberbullying and human trafficking, we can protect our youth and foster a healthier, more supportive community. Let's commit to making a difference, one step at a time.

Investigating the North Fox Island Pedophile Ring

The law and sentencing guidelines for those charged with abusing children are pretty strong. The justice system leans in the direction of giving the harshest sentences possible to those who are guilty of taking part in anything detrimental to a child's mental and physical well-being. As a retired detective, I recognize that more laws, harsher statutes, and stiffer penalties are considered the solution by several prosecutors, victim advocates, and individuals who have never seen first-hand the harm that pedophiles can inflict upon innocent children. Unfortunately, statistics prove that these increases in laws, tighter regulations, and stiffer penalties (and continued increases in the cost of maintaining compliance with these regulations) do not stop sex offenders from targeting unsuspecting minors. Every day, online detectives (or internet child safety consultants) capture child predators who want nothing more than to meet children in person and cause irreparable damage to these innocent individuals.

Most people are aware of the fact that pedophiles prey on children who are innocent and defenseless. The mere mention of the despicable act that these criminals engage in through possessing and distributing child pornography, luring unsuspecting children, making legitimate contact with underage kids, conducting illegal activities involving sex, etc., makes many people angry. What may not be comprehended by everyone is that the damage these pedophiles do can range from severe social anxiety and fear of physical contact to suicidal thoughts and complete self-destruction for those young individuals who are sexually exploited. There are hundreds of stories about adults who have faced lifelong challenges dealing with the detrimental effects of undesirable contact with pedophiles during their youth.

By examining the pedophile organization and its activities, one can gain a greater understanding of the devastating nature of these activities and the problems and issues that need to be considered when engaging in broader discussions of child protection. John Lang was a resident of Nova Scotia who moved to Northern Michigan in the late 1950s. He then opened a car dealership and became a successful businessman. Lang had a charismatic personality and later ran for State House of Commons. According to some people in town, Lang's friendly demeanor made it easy for him to communicate with people. This communication made the children feel friendly about him because several mothers let their children work for him.

In Northern Michigan, the story of a group of wealthy men who committed horrific acts of abuse known as the North Fox Island Ring has largely faded from public knowledge. This article takes an in-depth look at this largely untold story. Adam Starchild, commander of North Fox Island, recruited local children for trips or summer work on the island. This recruitment involved presenting the island as a utopia where food, money, sex, and the safety of its children were ensured. A comprehensive understanding of what victims faced as a result of the North Fox Island Pedophile Ring and subsequent fraud/corruption of the legal system is necessary to protect children in the future adequately.

My purpose with this Chapter is to analyze the North Fox Island pedophile ring and its connections to the broader network. My objectives include providing historical context as well as methodologically applying the concept of pedophile rings, of which there is a lack of academic literature. I will incorporate a broad range of historical cases in the analysis to show commonalities and differences among the various cases. The ultimate aim of the paper is to extend the literature on pedophile rings, addressing critical contemporary issues of child abuse and sex enslavement. Furthermore, this paper serves as the basis for my dissertation, which will include additional informal interviews. I want this paper to illustrate events that occurred in the past that are connected to instances today, recognizing that one has a similar genesis as the previous case. The scope of this paper is not a comparison to a defense of pedophilia and supports the actions taken to criminalize child abuse.

North Fox Island is a small private island located off the coast of Northwest Michigan between Beaver Island and the Leelanau Peninsula. The island is also situated almost equidistant from Traverse City and Charlevoix, two popular towns along the banks of Grand Traverse Bay. In March 1975, fewer than eight months after the disappearance of three Michigan State University students was showcased on the popular national show Good Morning America, the people of Michigan were introduced to what would become one of our state's most vile, dangerous, and underreported stories - a ring of Michigan pedophiles operating out of the desolate and publicly uninhabited Fox Islands. Long considered shocking allegations by the uninitiated and conspiracy theories by the influential individuals they involve, the disturbing stories rapidly began to circulate within the once-sleepy forests and topography of Northern and Lower Michigan, carried in from the remote intersections of several small town high schools, many of whom never wore their student body sizes with anything close to pride before the delivery of southbound and northbound buses from miles of gravel road cleared them of their burdens.

While in a relatively limited and minimally technological manner, the sexual abuse of children by adults has likely occurred for thousands of years in settings ranging from families, schools, churches, organizations, and networks of adults sharing a unilateral sexual preference – pedophilia - involving children of the same or the opposite sex. The origins and enactment of contemporary legislation, including so-called "Megan's Law" initiatives, reflect widespread concern over the proliferation of "official" sites and institutions that facilitate access to children. Economic opportunity, validated by the rise of Internet communications and avatars, contributes to the perception that the sexual abuse of children is a modern, frequently impersonal "business" without expenses or financial consequences. Tragically, it is possible that the ease of access to depictions of the sexual abuse of children, along

181

with the unprecedented expressiveness of online communication, could stimulate yet another developmental regressive stage by individuals who currently have limited or no sexual interest in children.

Over the past few decades, recognition of the significant psychological, emotional, and behavioral effects of childhood sexual abuse has motivated extensive research and considerable political activity directed toward its prevention and treatment. It has been assumed that the abuse of children, along with the production, distribution, and use of child pornography (visual depictions of the sexual abuse of children), is a relatively recent phenomenon, occurring primarily (if not exclusively) within the last few decades.

The nomadic ped kicked back on sofas watching gay porn on VHS tapes while they casually and openly abused a boy's mind, his heart, and his soul as the VCR purred softly. According to Nicolson, much of what has become known as gay liberation was really about the tolerance of man-boy pedophile relationships. Often, uninformed professionals and concerned lay people hastily affirm gay libber advances as benefiting the man-boy interests who masked their child abuse while linking their compromises to civil rights. Thus, pedophiles have said that we liberated queer pedophiles, but we implicitly huddle near the closet. The following century had dawned, and as many of our societal forms proved false, the ped head emerged.

The professional literature on the dynamics, structure, and social function of pedophile rings that emerged in the years following the publication of Formation of Character by The Mattachine Society in 1951 is seriously lacking. Freschi suggested that the sexual deviance of grown men toward teenage boys—usually boys entering puberty—is a conscious participation in a small but growing counter-culture based on the belief that sex between grown men and adolescent boys is socially and morally acceptable. This subculture appears to be based primarily on a relatively high degree of anonymity. Ken Plummer suggested that counter-cultures serve as an ideal human shield hiding criminal behavior and thus enabling pedophiles to meet and engage in both the truth and consequences of their deficits. Such counter-cultures were conceived as thoughts of sit-ins—"ped-in"—that defined and established an insulating community attracting like-minded perverts.

During the period 1969-1975, Francis D. Shelden operated an intricate network of ephebophiles in three states - Michigan, Illinois, and California. The primary sites were two villages in Michigan, a complex called North Fox Island in Lake Michigan, and an exclusive mid-Michigan resort. The "hebephilic genre" of the ring was approximately 12 to 16 years old and then seemed to focus on 14-year-olds. The American hebephile network of the 60s and 70s was composed of several parallel subnetworks and "private" nexus, each of which had a hematopoietic relationship with others. Most American hebephiles were tied to one or two primary contacts, but a few had essential relationships with others. On the marches were video production and the creation of specialty stores. There was also solid evidence of the importance of this group in the machinations of the significant U.S. hebephile circuit.

While the main focus of this study has been to investigate the North Fox Island pedophile ring, it is necessary to cover the features of this topic briefly. From an essential historical perspective, the North Fox Island pedophile operation was an "outgrowth" of a significant turning point in the development of the American Boylove movement. This ring was not only an integral part of the more extensive network of pederasty in the United States. Still, it was also the epicenter of significant legality, legislative, and law enforcement actions at a critical juncture in the growth (or devolution) of the Boylove movement. In addition, the mastermind of the North Fox Island operation, Francis D. Shelden, was not only a personal observer of the chain of events but was also a participant in the larger group at the forefront of the Boy/Man/Bondage movement.

The subsequent investigations, initially handled by Michigan and the FBI, led to Green (the mastermind he once boasted), the long-time gun and drug runner for his followers, and to Budd, among them, in addition to Richard's father's arrest. Those first two beached in California but were the children from Grand Traverse and Charlevoix Counties whom Green had taken with him over the past decade who, on returning, told their grim stories, which told the state and Federal investigators that there were many others and that the victims told credible tales. When searches and interviews began to uncover the gruesome details of what went on at Green's out-of-state haunts, protective parents took their children's stories of personal commerce, grass-stained clothing, skeet shooting, and sexual experiences to the parents who for years had used airplane rides to out-state cities as an innocent treat their children would generally seek from the beneficent pilaster.

This pedophile ring came to be uncovered purely by chance, as are most such criminal activities. The son of a North Fox Island neighbor, twelve-year-old Richard, informed his father in 1976 that he had been traveling with Green on Piper aircraft to Spokane (Washington), Richmond and Ann Arbor (Michigan), Washington, D.C., and other sites. His father called the police. Richard's mother called the FBI. The father attempted to protect his son but, reportedly against his son's wishes, tried to overcome the North Fox Island lookouts by quiet negotiation with them. The attempts failed, and because of them, charges were brought against him, which appear, since most have now been dropped, to have been intimidation against public disclosure of the activity as opposed to legal criminal charges.

Another individual who looms large in this case is past Michigan State Senator Alan Cropsey. In 1977, he was the Assistant Attorney General in charge of the office's Criminal Justice Division, and it was his office that prosecuted the second case that helped put Shelden away. BTSE had been approached by an individual who had heard about the outdoor, crossing-border events that the police and the state police would have been involved in had the arrest of a sex club madam in northern Michigan not been brought to a sudden, tragic halt. There was more biography than truth to the informant's story, but some of what was told seemed to have real possibilities. Several tractor-trailer rigs were parked in the parking lot of one of the amateur Demolition Derbies located outside Mt. Clemens. The trailers were gaudily painted and lettered, and they bore the name Healthy Education; the newspaper advertisement could be interpreted as 'what children do in this country.' The Healthy Education enterprise closed down quickly in the months to come. Still, the police would have closure in 1977 only if the past President of the

Police Officers Association had a large roll of hundred-dollar bills in his pocket.

The one sad truth that prevails is that a vast number of the victims of Shelden and Rick were foster children. Boys often seem to get shuffled off to private welfare agencies (because they need to have someone take them in, too), while girls go to foster homes. Many of the victims are gone. Some to drugs, a few were murdered, and many just disappeared. In the late 1970s and early 1980s, Shelden funded Martin Narren for sex and guns to take back Freedom, the black nation located in the Northwoods of Michigan that Shelden co-founded. Shelden also helped support Charles Blackmore until Blackmore murdered a boy in the 1970s.

Besides Francis Shelden, perhaps the most crucial figure in the North Fox Island pedophile ring was the traveling book salesman Neil Balkwell of Traverse City, who led the investigators to the island. Balkwell worked for Shelden under the names Richard Williams and Richard Erickson. He was also known as Richard Madden and was convicted in 1973 of criminal sexual conduct involving two boys. His son, Douglas Neil Balkwell, was victimized on the island in the summer of 1976, only to develop serious gambling problems as an adult and threaten the police that if he were not allowed to do as he pleased, they all would rot in hell when he released the true story of his life. Christopher Shelden, son of Shelden and Rick, was also a victim. Another important perpetrator was Gerald Dreher, who was a salesman for a company he named Healthy Education. Dreher sold sex paraphernalia and had people employed by Shelden (frequently paid prostitutes from the Detroit area) read his lectures to captive audiences in motels throughout the Detroit area. Dreher was important because he provided the victims who helped the police close the significant events in 1977 and 1978.

Collaboration sessions were held with a rock radio station to gauge audience interest in rabid commentary on prominent snuff participants as propaganda for the NFI club paradise. Together, they played snuff films in the radio viewers' minds and boasted of how the victims of sexual torture begged for a bullet in the forehead. John D. Andrews, the NFL's chairman of the board, was the radio host and the non-stop grin for the film. William Fox was the vice-president of his father's

Fox Island Corporation and the NFI Corporation. With L.T. Roe, the President of both corporations, the power struggle between Ben Dover and Rich Nutts, 2 NFI print club corrupters, ended in their oyster. The official charges were tax court evasion. Although many formed close ties and an advanced business partnership at a children's camp, there are no records of current business activities concerning the NFI batch exchange. The means of maintaining NFI documentation were dependent on police cooperation. Interviews with offenders and a search of the files of the Mason County system proved that police support dissolved to insubordination when the piques a flap would love. With a strong background in promoting baby-loving lodges for chit swap, up hopeless cock duress naive-tavern Zundels, hired a non-attorney, and transferred all business, authorship, money, investments, Lieber Vision control, etc., to Blushing sparrows are next's first venture was the restoration of the established zesty-gram billing system and address list. They would frequent large gatherings of pedophiles to exchange the petite-up-under-secret passwords with other activities. The last known secretive operation, beached at their prison boat, was the Stabbing Gopher. After acquiring the faded Cheshire smile from any medical or pharmaceutical sources, Officer Andrew Lee probably killed many other pedophile organizations. After his three years in prison ended, he went the other way.

The pedophile ring evolved slowly and meticulously. Users of the North Fox Island Corporation were encouraged to invest in the island with a like-minded interest in boys. Once the children arrived, membership to NFI took the form of a pyramid system or time-share membership with cabins built by John Robert Greene. There were 59 NFI memberships sold, and after a tour of other urban pedophile clubs, they protected each other's privacy and activities. The boys were enticed onto the planes with trips around the Lake Michigan island setting. The pilots, aided by navigational lights installed on the cabin windows, made flights to numerous isolated islands of Lake Michigan to pick up boys. These virgin boys were introduced to homosexuality and snuff films and also confined to continued exploitation and future production of snuff. One witness reports that Frank, a police officer, and Toby would disarm the children by caressing their chests and making them feel important. All child casualties would be disposed of at sea. After several years and some near apprehensions, there was an eventual falling out between the group. Many involved died in the next three years.

Other costs, felt by the entire society, also arise from the actions of the pedophiles. Throughout the sexual abuse, the environment surrounding the nudist camp and the ISGP Academy, as well as at summer camp, was degraded immensely. Hundreds of boys were lured to the farms and islands with the express purpose of using them for sexual gratification. An abuse of trust took place, as the boys came there with the expectation of a school or camp with the promise of new activities. The ISGP Academy and summer camp, instead, were turned into a place of horror and nightmare. The land, owned by members of the pedophile ring, was gradually turned from its original pristine state into farms surrounded by logged lands (on Beaver Island) and hunting ranges (on North Fox Island), where the boys could be potentially sexually molested without attracting the attention of authorities or parents.

The criminal activity that the North Fox Island defendants undertook had numerous and varied effects and consequences. An immediate one was the impact on their victims. These men abused hundreds of boys. Many testimonials have already been collected describing the psychological and emotional devastation that the victims suffered, including feelings of distrust of others, concerns over intimacy, inability to relate to and maintain normal sexual and interpersonal relations, feelings of loss of self-worth, self-blame and guilt, depression, anxiety, embarrassment, fear of ridicule, fear of their tendencies to abuse others, social ostracization, familial problems, substance abuse, and suicide attempts. These feelings and experiences of the victims will undoubtedly be further developed in any civil suits they bring against their abusers.

The one fascinating offshoot of North Fox Island is the survivors and the term victims, as many people would like to see abused boys as not victims. Outside of two living victims, John Robison and his brother, on the same day when Diskin arrested John's brother, he also found the foster family in Chicago. The victim had been a foster child with this wonderful family. They had nothing to do with the abuse and would have rewarded the boy and punished the pedophile. Diskin carried their brother to his squad car and told the family that the other boy was always running away. The brother went to a location near where Mr. X and Ken Schreyer put up John Robison's father one day one year earlier. Diskin told the foster parents to call him as soon as the boy returned. Diskin also used a list of names. Diskin paid a visit to Mr. X one day. Mr. X was the President of SCI-Systems Corporation, an island partner with Rand's B.C. deal, and a Cynewulf residence visitor to take C.P. pictures.

Michigan law proscribes a life sentence for kidnapping. Conspiracy to kidnap, or so-called kidnapping back in times before DNA collection became common, is a mandatory life sentence. The types of hands-on criminal sexual conduct crimes involved would cause the suspect to be a registered sex offender and be subject to community corrections monitoring if ever placed on parole. If a present-day search warrant on the island to look for dead bodies were to be executed, any surviving suspect would be subject to state criminal prosecution for the lack of video lottery insurance they maintained on their property. To cure these legal problems, the ACLU more recently suggested that sexual punishments should have been measured via coins instead of money in place of the videotaping of the sexual encounter. If anything is ever made, it looks like a nomination for a Nobel "science" prize. The presently deceased remaining suspect, however, will never stand before a judge since no crime is believed to have been committed by that individual. Regardless of where the evidence in the case leads, evidence development is essential so history may be set straight.

In recent news stories, law enforcement officials claimed that the original investigation had been extensive. History shows that many, if not most, of the victims were not interviewed during the original investigation; indeed, even in 2009, when the plan was blueprinted, it appears many victims would remain unknown and unaccounted for. Law enforcement officials have always been vehement that there are no innocent victims unaccounted for. The most recent news article states that 50 new possible victims have been identified, and several are retired law enforcement investigators. The 2009 investigation plan states that the law enforcement officials involved with victim identification would do a warm hand-off to an investigator familiar with the history.

The consequences are staggering. Objective evidence exists that elements of our government have been involved in large-scale service provision to a highly organized group of serious sex offenders. If local opinions of wealthy, well-connected men abusing minors are to be discounted, perhaps the disturbing increase of pedophile lobbying in the halls of Congress might not be grounds for alarm. However, we should be alarmed. Incredibly alarmed. To help the victims of North Fox Island seek justice, commentary following in future articles will focus on government investigations and prosecutions. There truly is another item of significance mentioned in the patterns of behavior of Balough, Miller, and Dyer. Their behavior is exactly that of the cultural child molester archetype, repeating patterns precisely described where they engage in a sex offense.

Coincidences cannot be employed as evidence in logical arguments. The use of any logical fallacy invalidates the argument. However, proper research demonstrates that people and events surrounding the North Fox Island pedophile ring are replete with improbable coincidences. These cannot be dismissed as a string of silly errors. A group of conscientious government agents, acting without coordination, could not muster this level of bungling. Believing they did would require us to embrace a second improbable supposition. Therefore, the logical conclusion is that, as hard as it may be to believe, the North Fox Island pedophile ring was the work of professionals, acting as components of a single organization, all aimed at a common goal. Few other organizations on the face of the earth can bring about this level of coordination with absolute assurance of the activities and reliability of its agents.

It is known that North Fox Island served as the base for Shelden's Brother Paul's Children's Mission while it was in operation. However, the thousands of photographs and lists of crossed-out names discovered seem far too voluminous for a small operation, as Shelden's Brother Paul's Children's Mission has been described. With the vast amount of subpoenaed photographs and lists of crossed-out names, we also discovered ledger books, financial statements, bank deposit slips, transferrable bank endorsements, checks, signed banknotes, tax receipts, blank Vatican Visas, and extensive personal correspondence. These provide a comprehensive view of the criminal activities perpetrated by John Norman Dunning and Francis Shelden. We are now in the process of entering these and affirming metadata into spreadsheets in the hope that other examples of their criminal activities in the United States and abroad may be discovered and disclosed.

During our study of the North Fox Island pedophile ring, we have found substantial evidence that the three men who were indicted are likely to have been part of a much larger organization of child exploiters. We have also found evidence that the true scope of this network was only partially uncovered during the original investigation. The extensive data of hand-recorded lists discovered in the John Dunning and Francis Shelden collections at Beloit College museums may lead to additional discoveries of people who exploited children in the United States and abroad at that time.

From a purely investigative and assessment standpoint, the North Fox Island case raises a variety of salient concerns. Many American child molesters circumvent state and federal reporting laws by seeking out appropriate victims in a large and populated area. Typically, by selecting meeting places such as shopping centers, amusement parks, and skating rinks, such sexual predators take their abuse away from the homes of the children they choose. Interestingly, this was not the behavior of the pedophile ring organized by John Powell. Collecting boys from at least a dozen different states and both coasts, the organized sexual abuse activities occurred on an isolated Midwestern Island accessible only by boat. This case presents an atypical travel scenario. By any standard, this fact presents a unique and likely unparalleled travel investigative opportunity.

Though the North Fox Island case occurred over thirty years ago, numerous compelling reasons exist to reevaluate this abomination. Such a reassessment is particularly timely considering the unvarnished cynicism of current public opinion concerning mass media portrayals of known and excessive incidents of explicit sexual abuse in contemporary American society. This exploitation has led to the false generalization that all victims of child sexual abuse become dysfunctional adults engaged in numerous inappropriate legal dealings. While patently incorrect, such conclusions have been mainly exploited within the more significant "repressed memory syndrome" field. This denial is especially ironic given the fact of our continually improving methodological techniques in child abuse and abuse-related assessment and evaluation.

The Hidden Veil

As we conclude this journey, it is imperative to confront the harrowing truths that have been unveiled. Forces indeed lead the world that many would instead remain ignorant of—forces that thrive in shadows, manipulating the fabric of our reality with sinister intent. Pedophiles and Satanists, hidden in plain sight, orchestrate ceremonies that are as ancient as they are malevolent. These are not mere myths or the fanciful musings of the paranoid; they are stark realities that have persisted for thousands of years.

Black magic is not a relic of bygone eras or a creation of overactive imaginations. It is a dark art that venerates the embodiment of evil—Satan, Lucifer, the Prince of Darkness, and their legion of the damned. These forces exist, interwoven into the very fabric of our society, influencing events and lives in overt and insidious ways. Today, satanic ceremonies continue to take place, shrouded in secrecy yet leaving their mark on the world.

If you seek validation, ask any honest priest or a truthful member of law enforcement. They will attest to the existence of these dark practices. This is not merely occult literature written to thrill or horrify—this is reality. People genuinely believe in these dark powers. The Church of Satan is publicly acknowledged, but what transpires in the clandestine gatherings is far more appalling and repulsive than one can imagine.

The actual black mass, an event cloaked in secrecy, defies comprehension. It is an abomination, a ritual so vile and depraved that words fail to encapsulate its horror. David and I have delved into the occult, driven to uncover and understand these truths. Through our interactions, we have met individuals who claim to be Satanists, those who profess knowledge and involvement in black magic. Their revelations are chilling, their conviction undeniable.

We hope these pages have entertained you and ignited a spark of curiosity, prompting you to question and explore these dark corners of existence on your own. This is more than a narrative; it is a warning—a plea for vigilance. Do not cross this dangerous line; the price is your mind and soul.

In the end, remember that knowledge is power. Arm yourself with awareness and discernment. The forces of darkness thrive on ignorance and fear. By shedding light on these hidden truths, we can diminish their influence and reclaim the sanctity of our world.

Stay vigilant. Stay informed. The veil has been lifted—never let it fall back into place.

In the realm of shadows, where darkness creeps,
In the Devil's Playground, where terror sleeps,
Innocence trembles, in the face of night,
As predators prowl, hidden from sight.
Their laughter tainted, by the sinister game,
Leaving scars that whisper, of unspeakable pain.
Trust shattered, like glass upon the ground,
In the Devil's Playground, despair is found.
Bright eyes dimmed, by fear's chilling embrace,
Echoes of silent screams, in the empty space.
Yet amidst the darkness, a flicker of light,
Courage and love, to banish the night.
United we stand, against the evil tide,
Guiding the innocent, with hearts open wide.
In the Devil's Playground, we take our stand,
Protecting the vulnerable, hand in hand.
With strength and resolve, we face the fight,
Against the demons that haunt the night.
In the Devil's Playground, our mission clear,
To bring hope and salvation to those held dear.

Printed in the United States
by Baker & Taylor Publisher Services